EQUUS

One of the foremost dramatists of our time, Peter Shaffer was born in Liverpool and educated at St Paul's School and Trinity College, Cambridge. He had several varied jobs before earning fame as a playwright – working as a 'Bevin Boy' in the coal mines during the Second World War, in the acquisitions department of the New York Public Library and for the London music-publishing firm of Boosey & Hawkes.

His first big success came in 1958 with *Five Finger Exercise*. The play ran for nearly two years at the Comedy Theatre in London, won the *Evening Standard* Drama Award and was subsequently presented, with great acclaim, in New York City. Other Shaffer successes include *The Private Ear: The Public Eye* (which, like *Lettice and Lovage*, starred Maggie Smith and played at the Globe Theatre); *The Royal Hunt of the Sun*, an epic drama concerning the Spanish conquest of the Inca Empire; the hilarious farce, *Black Comedy*; *The Battle of Shrivings*; *Equus*, a sensational triumph in London and in New York where it received the 1975 Tony Award for Best Play of the year; and *Amadeus*, which also won the same prize, as well as the 1979 *Evening Standard* Drama Award, the Plays and Players Award, and the London Theatre Critics' Award. Both these last mentioned plays boast the rare distinction of having run for over a thousand performances on Broadway, and in 1984 the film of *Amadeus* won the Academy Award for both script and picture. His most recent plays are *Yonadab*, *Lettice and Lovage* which received the *Evening Standard* Drama Award for the best comedy of 1988, and *The Gift of the Gorgon*. Penguin publish a number of his plays. Peter Shaffer was awarded the CBE in the 1987 Birthday Honours List.

PETER SHAFFER

*

EQUUS

Penguin Books

PENGUIN BOOKS

Published by the Penguin Group
Penguin Books Ltd, 27 Wrights Lane, London W8 5TZ, England
Penguin Books USA Inc., 375 Hudson Street, New York, New York 10014, USA
Penguin Books Australia Ltd, Ringwood, Victoria, Australia
Penguin Books Canada Ltd, 10 Alcorn Avenue, Toronto, Ontario, Canada M4V 3B2
Penguin Books (NZ) Ltd, 182–190 Wairau Road, Auckland 10, New Zealand

Penguin Books Ltd, Registered Offices: Harmondsworth, Middlesex, England

Equus first published by André Deutsch 1973
First published in the United States of America by Atheneum 1974
First published in Penguin Books in a collection with *Five Finger Exercise* and *Shrivings* 1976
Published in Penguin Books as a separate play 1977
25 27 29 30 28 26

Printed in England by Clays Ltd, St Ives plc
Set in Monotype Bembo

FOR PAUL
WITH LOVE

A NOTE ON THE TEXT

WHAT appears in this text is a description of the first production of *Equus* at the National Theatre in July 1973. In making this description, I am partly satisfying myself, but also partly bowing to demand.

When people buy the published text of a new play, they mostly want to recall the experience they received in the theatre. That experience is composed, of course, not merely of the words they heard, but the gestures they saw, and the lighting, and the look of the thing.

There are, however, evils attendant on this sort of description. It can imprison a play in one particular stylization. Just as seriously, it can do a real injustice to the original Director, by incorporating his ideas without truly acknowledging them. Worse, if the Director is as inventive as John Dexter, it can actually seem to minimize those ideas, just by flatly setting down on paper what was far from flat on the stage, and listing inexpressively details of his work which, in accumulation, became deeply expressive.

Dexter directs powerfully through suggestion. Into the theatrical spaces he contrives, flows the communal imagination of an audience. He enables it to charge the action of a play with electric life. He is a master of gesture and of economy. Aesthetically, his founding fathers are Noh Drama and Berthold Brecht: the plain plank; the clear light; the great pleasure in a set-piece. I do not mean by this that he would ever direct a single minute of physical action which detracted from the meaning of a play, or in some grand visual sense subverted it – he sharply dislikes effect isolated from context – but he is naturally and rightly drawn to plays which demand elaborate physical actions to complete them.

The Royal Hunt of the Sun and *Black Comedy*, both of which he directed, are such pieces: and so is *Equus*. Their visual action is to me as much a part of the play as the dialogue. I suppose my head has always been full of images. The gold masks staring hopefully and then in gathering despair at the sky, at the end of *The Royal Hunt of the Sun*, had been part of my imagination ever since I first saw a Peruvian funeral mask with its elongated eyes and red-smeared cheeks. Brindsley Miller in the lit-up darkness of *Black Comedy*, slowly moving the spiky legs of a Regency chair one inch before the innocent face of his spinster neighbour, had tiptoed that very journey in my head as I sat at my desk. But such images, like the Field of Ha-ha in *Equus* with its mist and nettles, still have to be externalized. In John Dexter's courageous and precise staging, they acquire a vibrant and unforgettable life.

While I am confessing debts, let me mention John Napier who created the tough, bright masks of horsedom; Andy Phillips who lit them superbly; and above all, Claude Chagrin, who animated them. She created, with the help of six human actors, a stable of Superhorses to stalk through the mind.

Finally, out of a fine company I must set down the names of three actors who made the first performance of this play live with a very special intensity. Alec McCowen's Dysart touched audiences deeply with its dry agony. Peter Firth's Alan left them sighing with admiration. Nicholas Clay's horse Nugget was, quite simply, unforgettable.

Rehearsing a play is making the word flesh. Publishing a play is reversing the process. I can only hope this book is not too unjust to these brilliant people.

P.S.

A NOTE ON THE PLAY

ONE weekend over two years ago, I was driving with a friend through bleak countryside. We passed a stable. Suddenly he was reminded by it of an alarming crime which he had heard about recently at a dinner party in London. He knew only one horrible detail, and his complete mention of it could barely have lasted a minute – but it was enough to arouse in me an intense fascination.

The act had been committed several years before by a highly disturbed young man. It had deeply shocked a local bench of magistrates. It lacked, finally, any coherent explanation.

A few months later my friend died. I could not verify what he had said, or ask him to expand it. He had given me no name, no place, and no time. I don't think he knew them. All I possessed was his report of a dreadful event, and the feeling it engendered in me. I knew very strongly that I wanted to interpret it in some entirely personal way. I had to create a mental world in which the deed could be made comprehensible.

Every person and incident in *Equus* is of my own invention, save the crime itself; and even that I modified to accord with what I feel to be acceptable theatrical proportion. I am grateful now that I have never received confirmed details of the real story, since my concern has been more and more with a different kind of exploration.

I have been lucky, in doing final work on the play, to have enjoyed the advice and expert comment of a distinguished child psychiatrist. Through him I have tried to keep things real in a more naturalistic sense. I have also come to perceive that psychiatrists are an immensely varied breed, professing immensely varied methods and techniques. Martin Dysart is simply one doctor in one hospital. I must take responsibility for him, as I do for his patient.

P.S.

EQUUS

Characters:

MARTIN DYSART, *a psychiatrist*
ALAN STRANG
FRANK STRANG, *his father*
DORA STRANG, *his mother*
HESTHER SALOMON, *a magistrate*
JILL MASON
HARRY DALTON, *a stable owner*
A YOUNG HORSEMAN
A NURSE

SIX ACTORS – *including the Young Horseman, who also plays Nugget –*
appear as Horses.

Equus was first presented by The National Theatre at The Old Vic
Theatre on 26 July 1973, with the following cast:

MARTIN DYSART	Alec McCowen
NURSE	Louie Ramsay
HESTHER SALOMON	Gillian Barge
ALAN STRANG	Peter Firth
FRANK STRANG	Alan MacNaughtan
DORA STRANG	Jeanne Watts
HORSEMAN	Nicholas Clay
HARRY DALTON	David Healy

THE CHARACTERS

JILL MASON   Doran Godwin
and
Neil Cunningham, David Graham, David Kincaid, Maggie Riley,
Rosalind Shanks, Veronica Sowerby, Harry Waters

PRODUCTION   John Dexter
DESIGN   John Napier
MUSIC   Marc Wilkinson
LIGHTING   Andy Phillips
MOVEMENT   Claude Chagrin
ASSISTANT TO THE PRODUCER   Kenneth Mackintosh
STAGE MANAGER   Diana Boddington
DEPUTY STAGE MANAGERS   Phil Robins
                                              Tony Walters
ASSISTANT STAGE MANAGERS   Elizabeth Markham
                                              Terry Oliver

*The main action of the play takes place in Rokesby Psychiatric Hospital in
southern England. The time is the present.*

*The play is divided into numbered scenes, indicating a change of time or
locale or mood. The action, however, is continuous.*

THE SETTING

A SQUARE of wood set on a circle of wood.

The square resembles a railed boxing ring. The rail, also of wood,
encloses three sides. It is perforated on each side by an opening. Under
the rail are a few vertical slats, as if in a fence. On the downstage side
there is no rail. The whole square is set on ball bearings, so that by
slight pressure from actors standing round it on the circle, it can be
made to turn round smoothly by hand.

On the square are set three little plain benches, also of wood. They
are placed parallel with the rail, against the slats, but can be moved out
by the actors to stand at right angles to them.

Set into the floor of the square, and flush with it, is a thin metal
pole, about a yard high. This can be raised out of the floor, to stand
upright. It acts as a support for the actor playing Nugget, when he is
ridden.

In the area outside the circle stand benches. Two downstage left and
right are curved to accord with the circle. The left one is used by
Dysart as a listening and observing post when he is out of the square,
and also by Alan as his hospital bed. The right one is used by Alan's
parents, who sit side by side on it. (Viewpoint is from the main body
of the audience.)

Further benches stand upstage, and accommodate the other actors.
All the cast of *Equus* sits on stage the entire evening. They get up to
perform their scenes, and return when they are done to their places
around the set. They are witnesses, assistants – and especially a Chorus.

Upstage, forming a backdrop to the whole, are tiers of seats in the
fashion of a dissecting theatre, formed into two railed-off blocks,
pierced by a central tunnel. In these blocks sit members of the audience. During the play, Dysart addresses them directly from time to

time, as he addresses the main body of the theatre. No other actor ever refers to them.

To left and right, downstage, stand two ladders on which are suspended horse masks.

The colour of all benches is olive green.

Above the stage hangs a battery of lights, set in a huge metal ring. Light cues, in this version, will be only of the most general description.

THE HORSES

THE actors wear track-suits of chestnut velvet. On their feet are light strutted hooves, about four inches high, set on metal horse-shoes. On their hands are gloves of the same colour. On their heads are tough masks made of alternating bands of silver wire and leather; their eyes are outlined by leather blinkers. The actors' own heads are seen beneath them: no attempt should be made to conceal them.

Any literalism which could suggest the cosy familiarity of a domestic animal – or worse, a pantomime horse – should be avoided. The actors should never crouch on all fours, or even bend forward. They must always – except on the one occasion where Nugget is ridden – stand upright, as if the body of the horse extended invisibly behind them. Animal effect must be created entirely mimetically, through the use of legs, knees, neck, face, and the turn of the head which can move the mask above it through all the gestures of equine wariness and pride. Great care must also be taken that the masks are put on before the audience with very precise timing – the actors watching each other, so that the masking has an exact and ceremonial effect.

THE CHORUS

REFERENCES are made in the text to the Equus Noise. I have in mind a choric effect, made by all the actors sitting round upstage, and composed of humming, thumping, and stamping – though never of neighing or whinnying. This Noise heralds or illustrates the presence of Equus the God.

ACT ONE

Darkness.
Silence.
Dim light up on the square. In a spotlight stands ALAN STRANG, *a lean boy of seventeen, in sweater and jeans. In front of him, the horse* NUGGET. ALAN's *pose represents a contour of great tenderness: his head is pressed against the shoulder of the horse, his hands stretching up to fondle its head. The horse in turn nuzzles his neck.*
The flame of a cigarette lighter jumps in the dark. Lights come up slowly on the circle. On the left bench, downstage, MARTIN DYSART, *smoking. A man in his mid-forties.*

DYSART: With one particular horse, called Nugget, he embraces. The animal digs its sweaty brow into his cheek, and they stand in the dark for an hour - like a necking couple. And of all nonsensical things - I keep thinking about the *horse*! Not the boy: the horse, and what it may be trying to do. I keep seeing that huge head kissing him with its chained mouth. Nudging through the metal some desire absolutely irrelevant to filling its belly or propagating its own kind. What desire could that be? Not to stay a horse any longer? Not to remain reined up for ever in those particular genetic strings? Is it possible, at certain moments we cannot imagine, a horse can add its sufferings together - the non-stop jerks and jabs that are its daily life - and turn them into grief? What use is grief to a horse?

[ALAN *leads* NUGGET *out of the square and they disappear together up the tunnel, the horse's hooves scraping delicately on the wood.*

DYSART *rises, and addresses both the large audience in the theatre and the smaller one on stage.*]

You see, I'm lost. What use, I should be asking, are questions like these to an overworked psychiatrist in a provincial hospital? They're worse than useless; they are, in fact, subversive.

[*He enters the square. The light grows brighter.*]

The thing is, I'm desperate. You see, I'm wearing that horse's head myself. That's the feeling. All reined up in old language and old assumptions, straining to jump clean-hoofed on to a whole new track of being I only suspect is there. I can't see it, because my educated, average head is being held at the wrong angle. I can't jump because the bit forbids it, and my own basic force – my horse-power, if you like – is too little. The only thing I know for sure is this: a horse's head is finally unknowable to me. Yet I handle children's heads – which I must presume to be more complicated, at least in the area of my chief concern . . . In a way, it has nothing to do with this boy. The doubts have been there for years, piling up steadily in this dreary place. It's only the extremity of this case that's made them active. I know that. The *extremity* is the point! All the same, whatever the reason, they are now, these doubts, not just vaguely worrying – but intolerable . . . I'm sorry. I'm not making much sense. Let me start properly; in order. It began one Monday last month, with Hesther's visit.

2

[*The light gets warmer.*
He sits. NURSE *enters the square.*]

NURSE: Mrs Salomon to see you, Doctor.

DYSART: Show her in, please.

[NURSE *leaves and crosses to where* HESTHER *sits.*]

Some days I blame Hesther. She brought him to me. But of course that's nonsense. What is he but a last straw? a last symbol? If it hadn't been him, it would have been the next patient, or the next. At least, I suppose so.

[HESTHER *enters the square: a woman in her mid-forties.*]

HESTHER: Hallo, Martin.

[DYSART *rises and kisses her on the cheek.*]

DYSART: Madam Chairman! Welcome to the torture chamber!

HESTHER: It's good of you to see me right away.

DYSART: You're a welcome relief. Take a couch.

HESTHER: It's been a day?

DYSART: No – just a fifteen-year-old schizophrenic, and a girl of eight thrashed into catatonia by her father. Normal, really ... You're in a state.

HESTHER: Martin, this is the most shocking case I ever tried.

DYSART: So you said on the phone.

HESTHER: I mean it. My bench wanted to send the boy to prison. For life, if they could manage it. It took me two hours solid arguing to get him sent to you instead.

DYSART: Me?

HESTHER: I mean, to hospital.

DYSART: Now look, Hesther. Before you say anything else, I can take no more patients at the moment. I can't even cope with the ones I have.

HESTHER: You must.

DYSART: Why?

HESTHER: Because most people are going to be disgusted by the whole thing. Including doctors.

DYSART: May I remind you I share this room with two highly competent psychiatrists?

HESTHER: Bennett and Thoroughgood. They'll be as shocked as the public.

DYSART: That's an absolutely unwarrantable statement.

HESTHER: Oh, they'll be cool and exact. And underneath they'll be revolted, and immovably English. Just like my bench.

DYSART: Well, what am I? Polynesian?

19

HESTHER: You know exactly what I mean! ... [*Pause.*] Please, Martin. It's vital. You're this boy's only chance.

DYSART: Why? What's he done? Dosed some little girl's Pepsi with Spanish Fly? What could possibly throw your bench into two-hour convulsions?

HESTHER: He blinded six horses with a metal spike.

[*A long pause.*]

DYSART: Blinded?

HESTHER: Yes.

DYSART: All at once, or over a period?

HESTHER: All on the same night.

DYSART: Where?

HESTHER: In a riding stable near Winchester. He worked there at week-ends.

DYSART: How old?

HESTHER: Seventeen.

DYSART: What did he say in Court?

HESTHER: Nothing. He just sang.

DYSART: Sang?

HESTHER: Any time anyone asked him anything.

[*Pause.*]

Please take him, Martin. It's the last favour I'll ever ask you.

DYSART: No, it's not.

HESTHER: No, it's not – and he's probably abominable. All I know is, he needs you badly. Because there really is nobody within a hundred miles of your desk who can handle him. And perhaps understand what this is about. Also ...

DYSART: What?

HESTHER: There's something very special about him.

DYSART: In what way?

HESTHER: Vibrations.

DYSART: You and your vibrations.

HESTHER: They're quite startling. You'll see.

DYSART: When does he get here?

HESTHER: Tomorrow morning. Luckily there was a bed in Neville

Ward. I know this is an awful imposition, Martin. Frankly I didn't know what else to do.

[*Pause.*]

DYSART: Can you come in and see me on Friday?

HESTHER: Bless you!

DYSART: If you come after work I can give you a drink. Will six thirty be all right?

HESTHER: You're a dear. You really are.

DYSART: Famous for it.

HESTHER: Goodbye.

DYSART: By the way, what's his name?

HESTHER: Alan Strang.

[*She leaves and returns to her seat.*]

DYSART [*to audience*]: What did I expect of him? Very little, I promise you. One more dented little face. One more adolescent freak. The usual unusual. One great thing about being in the adjustment business: you're never short of customers.

[NURSE *comes down the tunnel, followed by* ALAN. *She enters the square.*]

NURSE: Alan Strang, Doctor.

[*The boy comes in.*]

DYSART: Hallo. My name's Martin Dysart. I'm pleased to meet you.

[*He puts out his hand. Alan does not respond in any way.*]

That'll be all, Nurse, thank you.

3

[NURSE *goes out and back to her place.*
DYSART *sits, opening a file.*]

So: did you have a good journey? I hope they gave you lunch at least. Not that there's much to choose between a British Rail meal and one here.

[ALAN *stands staring at him.*]

DYSART: Won't you sit down?

[*Pause. He does not.* DYSART *consults his file.*]

Is this your full name? Alan Strang?

[*Silence.*]

And you're seventeen. Is that right? Seventeen? . . . Well?

ALAN [*singing low*]: Double your pleasure,
Double your fun
With Doublemint, Doublemint
Doublemint gum.

DYSART [*unperturbed*]: Now, let's see. You work in an electrical shop during the week. You live with your parents, and your father's a printer. What sort of things does he print?

ALAN [*singing louder*]: Double your pleasure
Double your fun
With Doublemint, Doublemint
Doublemint gum.

DYSART: I mean does he do leaflets and calendars? Things like that?

[*The boy approaches him, hostile.*]

ALAN [*singing*]: Try the taste of Martini
The most beautiful drink in the world.
It's the right one –
The bright one –
That's Martini!

DYSART: I wish you'd sit down, if you're going to sing. Don't you think you'd be more comfortable?

[*Pause.*]

ALAN [*singing*]: There's only one 'T' in Typhoo!
In packets and in teabags too.
Any way you make it, you'll find it's true:
There's only one 'T' in Typhoo!

DYSART [*appreciatively*]: Now that's a good song. I like it better than the other two. Can I hear that one again?

[ALAN *starts away from him, and sits on the upstage bench.*]

ALAN [*singing*]: Double your pleasure
Double your fun
With Doublemint, Doublemint
Doublemint gum.

DYSART [*smiling*]: You know I was wrong. I really do think that one's
better. It's got such a catchy tune. Please do that one again.

[*Silence. The boy glares at him.*]

I'm going to put you in a private bedroom for a little while. There
are one or two available, and they're rather more pleasant than
being in a ward. Will you please come and see me tomorrow? . . .
[*He rises.*] By the way, which parent is it who won't allow you to
watch television? Mother or father? Or is it both? [*Calling out of
the door.*] Nurse!

[ALAN *stares at him.* NURSE *comes in.*]

NURSE: Yes, Doctor?

DYSART: Take Strang here to Number Three, will you? He's moving
in there for a while.

NURSE: Very good, Doctor.

DYSART [*to* ALAN]: You'll like that room. It's nice.

[*The boy sits staring at* DYSART.

DYSART *returns the stare.*]

NURSE: Come along, young man. This way . . . I said this way,
please.

[*Reluctantly* ALAN *rises and goes to* NURSE, *passing dangerously
close to* DYSART, *and out through the left door.* DYSART *looks after
him, fascinated.*]

4

[NURSE *and patient move on to the circle, and walk downstage to the
bench where the doctor first sat, which is to serve also as* ALAN's *bed.*]

NURSE: Well now; isn't this nice? You're lucky to be in here, you
know, rather than the ward. That ward's a noisy old place.

ALAN [*singing*]: Let's go where you wanna go – Texaco!

NURSE [*contemplating him*]: I hope you're not going to make a nuisance of yourself. You'll have a much better time of it here, you know, if you behave yourself.

ALAN: Fuck off.

NURSE [*tight*]: That's the bell there. The lav's down the corridor.

[*She leaves him, and goes back to her place.*

ALAN *lies down.*]

5

[DYSART *stands in the middle of the square and addresses the audience He is agitated.*]

DYSART: That night, I had this very explicit dream. In it I'm a chief priest in Homeric Greece. I'm wearing a wide gold mask, all noble and bearded, like the so-called Mask of Agamemnon found at Mycenae. I'm standing by a thick round stone and holding a sharp knife. In fact, I'm officiating at some immensely important ritual sacrifice, on which depends the fate of the crops or of a military expedition. The sacrifice is a herd of children: about 500 boys and girls. I can see them stretching away in a long queue, right across the plain of Argos. I know it's Argos because of the red soil. On either side of me stand two assistant priests, wearing masks as well: lumpy, pop-eyed masks, such as also were found at Mycenae. They are enormously strong, these other priests, and absolutely tireless. As each child steps forward, they grab it from behind and throw it over the stone. Then, with a surgical skill which amazes even me, I fit in the knife and slice elegantly down to the navel, just like a seamstress following a pattern. I part the flaps, sever the inner tubes, yank them out and throw them hot and steaming on to the floor. The other two then study the pattern they make, as if they were reading hieroglyphics. It's obvious to me that I'm tops as chief priest. It's this unique talent for carving that has got me where I am. The only thing is, unknown to them, I've started to feel distinctly nauseous. And with each victim, it's getting worse. My face is going green behind the mask. Of course, I redouble my efforts to look professional – cutting and snipping for all I'm worth: mainly because I know that if ever those two assistants so much as glimpse my distress – and the implied doubt that this repetitive and smelly work is doing any social good at all – I will be the next across the stone. And then, of course – the damn mask begins to slip. The priests both turn and look at it – it slips some more – they see the green sweat running down my face – their gold pop-eyes suddenly fill up with blood – they tear the knife out of my hand . . . and I wake up.

6

[HESTHER *enters the square. Light grows warmer.*]

HESTHER: That's the most indulgent thing I ever heard.

DYSART: You think?

HESTHER: Please don't be ridiculous. You've done the most superb work with children. You must know that.

DYSART: Yes, but do the children?

HESTHER: Really!

DYSART: I'm sorry.

HESTHER: So you should be.

DYSART: I don't know why you listen. It's just professional menopause. Everyone gets it sooner or later. Except you.

HESTHER: Oh, of course. I feel totally fit to be a magistrate all the time.

DYSART: No, you don't – but then that's you feeling unworthy to fill a job. I feel the job is unworthy to fill me.

HESTHER: Do you seriously?

DYSART: More and more. I'd like to spend the next ten years wandering very slowly around the *real* Greece . . . Anyway, all this dream nonsense is your fault.

HESTHER: Mine?

DYSART: It's that lad of yours who started it off. Do you know it's his face I saw on every victim across the stone?

HESTHER: Strang?

DYSART: He has the strangest stare I ever met.

HESTHER: Yes.

DYSART: It's exactly like being accused. Violently accused. But what of? ... Treating him is going to be unsettling. Especially in my present state. His singing was direct enough. His speech is more so.

HESTHER [*surprised*]: He's talking to you, then?

DYSART: Oh yes. It took him two more days of commercials, and then he snapped. Just like that – I suspect it has something to do with his nightmares.

[NURSE *walks briskly round the circle, a blanket over her arm, a clipboard of notes in her hand.*]

HESTHER: He has nightmares?

DYSART: Bad ones.

NURSE: We had to give him a sedative or two, Doctor. Last night it was exactly the same.

DYSART [*to* NURSE]: What does he do? Call out?

NURSE [*to desk*]: A lot of screaming, Doctor.

DYSART [*to* NURSE]: Screaming?

NURSE: One word in particular.

DYSART [*to* NURSE]: You mean a special word?

NURSE: Over and over again. [*Consulting clipboard.*] It sounds like 'Ek'.

HESTHER: Ek?

NURSE: Yes, Doctor. Ek ... 'Ek!' he goes. 'Ek!'

HESTHER: How weird.

NURSE: When I woke him up he clung to me like he was going to break my arm.

[*She stops at* ALAN's *bed. He is sitting up. She puts the blanket over him, and returns to her place.*]

DYSART: And then he bursts in – just like that – without knocking or anything. Fortunately, I didn't have a patient with me.

ALAN [*jumping up*]: *Dad!*

HESTHER: What?

DYSART: The answer to a question I'd asked him two days before.
Spat out with the same anger as he sang the commercials.

HESTHER: Dad what?

ALAN: Who hates telly.

[*He lies downstage on the circle, as if watching television.*]

HESTHER: You mean his dad forbids him to watch?

DYSART: Yes.

ALAN: It's a dangerous drug.

HESTHER: Oh, really!

[FRANK *stands up and enters the scene downstage on the circle. A man
in his fifties.*]

FRANK [*to* ALAN]: It may not look like that, but that's what it is.
Absolutely fatal mentally, if you receive my meaning.

[DORA *follows him on. She is also middle aged.*]

DORA: That's a little extreme, dear, isn't it?

FRANK: You sit in front of that thing long enough, you'll become
stupid for life – like most of the population. [*To* ALAN.] The thing
is, it's a *swiz*. It seems to be offering you something, but actually
it's taking something away. Your intelligence and your concentra-
tion, every minute you watch it. That's a true swiz, do you see?

[*Seated on the floor,* ALAN *shrugs.*]

I don't want to sound like a spoilsport, old chum – but there really
is no substitute for reading. What's the matter; don't you like it?

ALAN: It's all right.

FRANK: I know you think it's none of my beeswax, but it really is you
know . . . Actually, it's a disgrace when you come to think of it.
You the son of a printer, and never opening a book! If all the
world was like you, I'd be out of a job, if you receive my meaning!

DORA: All the same, times change, Frank.

FRANK [*reasonably*]: They change if you let them change, Dora.
Please return that set in the morning.

ALAN [*crying out*]: No!

DORA: Frank! No!

FRANK: I'm sorry, Dora, but I'm not having that thing in the house a moment longer. I told you I didn't want it to begin with.

DORA: But, dear, everyone watches television these days!

FRANK: Yes, and what do they watch? Mindless violence! Mindless jokes! Every five minutes some laughing idiot selling you something you don't want, just to bolster up the economic system. [*To* ALAN.] I'm sorry, old chum.

[*He leaves the scene and sits again in his place.*]

HESTHER: He's a Communist, then?

DYSART: Old-type Socialist, I'd say. Relentlessly self-improving.

HESTHER: They're *both* older than you'd expect.

DYSART: So I gather.

DORA [*looking after* FRANK]: Really, dear, you are very extreme!

[*She leaves the scene too, and again sits beside her husband.*]

HESTHER: She's an ex-school teacher, isn't she?

DYSART: Yes. The boy's proud of that. We got on to it this afternoon.

ALAN [*belligerently, standing up*]: She knows more than you.

[HESTHER *crosses and sits by* DYSART. *During the following, the boy walks round the circle, speaking to* DYSART *but not looking at him.* DYSART *replies in the same manner.*]

DYSART [*to* ALAN]: Does she?

ALAN: I bet I do too. I bet I know more history than you.

DYSART [*to* ALAN]: Well, I bet you don't.

ALAN: All right: who was the Hammer of the Scots?

DYSART [*to* ALAN]: I don't know: who?

ALAN: King Edward the First. Who never smiled again?

DYSART [*to* ALAN]: I don't know: who?

ALAN: You don't know anything, do you? It was Henry the First. I know all the Kings.

DYSART [*to* ALAN]: And who's your favourite?

ALAN: John.

DYSART [*to* ALAN]: Why?

ALAN: Because he put out the eyes of that smarty little –

[*Pause.*]

[*Sensing he has said something wrong.*] Well, he didn't really. He was prevented, because the gaoler was merciful!

HESTHER: Oh dear.

ALAN: *He was prevented!*

DYSART: Something odder was to follow.

ALAN: Who said 'Religion is the opium of the people'?

HESTHER: Good Lord!

[ALAN *giggles.*]

DYSART: The odd thing was, he said it with a sort of guilty snigger. The sentence is obviously associated with some kind of tension.

HESTHER: What did you say?

DYSART: I gave him the right answer. [*To* ALAN.] Karl Marx.

ALAN: No.

DYSART [*to* ALAN]: Then who?

ALAN: Mind your own beeswax.

DYSART: It's probably his dad. He may say it to provoke his wife.

HESTHER: And you mean she's religious?

DYSART: She could be. I tried to discover – none too successfully.

ALAN: Mind your own beeswax!

[ALAN *goes back to bed and lies down in the dark.*]

DYSART: However, I shall find out on Sunday.

HESTHER: What do you mean?

DYSART [*getting up*]: I want to have a look at his home, so I invited myself over.

HESTHER: Did you?

DYSART: If there's any tension over religion, it should be evident on a Sabbath evening! I'll let you know.

[*He kisses her cheek and they part, both leaving the square.* HESTHER *sits in her place again;* DYSART *walks round the circle, and greets* DORA *who stands waiting for him downstage.*]

29

DYSART [*shaking hands*]: Mrs Strang.

DORA: Mr Strang's still at the Press, I'm afraid. He should be home in a minute.

DYSART: He works Sundays as well?

DORA: Oh, yes. He doesn't set much store by Sundays.

DYSART: Perhaps you and I could have a little talk before he comes in.

DORA: Certainly. Won't you come into the living-room?

[*She leads the way into the square. She is very nervous.*]

Please . . .

[*She motions him to sit, then holds her hands tightly together.*]

DYSART: Mrs Strang, have you any idea how this thing could have occurred?

DORA: I can't imagine, Doctor. It's all so unbelievable! . . . Alan's always been such a gentle boy. He loves animals! Especially horses.

DYSART: Especially?

DORA: Yes. He even has a photograph of one up in his bedroom. A beautiful white one, looking over a gate. His father gave it to him a few years ago, off a calendar he'd printed – and he's never taken it down . . . And when he was seven or eight, I used to have to read him the same book over and over, all *about* a horse.

DYSART: Really?

DORA: Yes; it was called Prince, and no one could ride him.

[*ALAN calls from his bed, not looking at his mother.*]

ALAN [*excited, younger voice*]: Why not? . . . Why not? . . . Say it! In his voice!

DORA: He loved the idea of animals talking.

DYSART: Did he?

ALAN: *Say it! Say it! . . . Use his voice!*

DORA ['*proud*' *voice*]: 'Because I am faithful!'

[*ALAN giggles.*]

'My name is Prince, and I'm a Prince among horses! Only my young Master can ride me! Anyone else – I'll *throw off*!'

[*ALAN giggles louder.*]

And then I remember I used to tell him a funny thing about falling off horses. Did you know that when Christian cavalry first appeared in the New World, the pagans thought <u>horse and rider</u> was one person?

DYSART: Really?

ALAN [*sitting up, amazed*]: One person?

DORA: Actually, they thought it must be a god.

ALAN: A *god!*

DORA: It was only when one rider fell off, they realized the truth.

DYSART: That's fascinating. I never heard that before ... Can you remember anything else like that you may have told him about horses?

DORA: Well, not really. They're in the Bible, of course. 'He saith among the trumpets, Ha, ha.'

DYSART: Ha, ha?

DORA: The Book of Job. Such a noble passage. *You* know – [*Quoting.*] 'Hast thou given the horse strength?'

ALAN [*responding*]: 'Hast thou clothed his neck with thunder?'

DORA [*to* ALAN]: 'The glory of his nostrils is terrible!'

ALAN: 'He swallows the ground with fierceness and rage!'

DORA: 'He saith among the trumpets –'

ALAN [*trumpeting*]: 'Ha! Ha!'

DORA [*to* DYSART]: Isn't that splendid?

DYSART: It certainly is.

ALAN [*trumpeting*]: Ha! Ha!

DORA: And then, of course, we saw an awful lot of Westerns on the television. He couldn't have enough of those.

DYSART: But surely you don't have a set, do you? I understood Mr Strang doesn't approve.

DORA [*conspiratorially*]: He doesn't ... I used to let him slip off in the afternoons to a friend next door.

DYSART [*smiling*]: You mean without his father's knowledge?

DORA: What <u>the eye does not see</u>, the heart does not <u>grieve over</u>, does it? Anyway, Westerns are harmless enough, surely?

[FRANK *stands up and enters the square.*

31

ALAN *lies back under the blanket.*]

[*To* FRANK.] Oh, hallo dear. This is Dr Dysart.

FRANK [*shaking hands*]: How d'you do?

DYSART: How d'you do?

DORA: I was just telling the Doctor, Alan's always adored horses.

FRANK [*tight*]: We assumed he did.

DORA: You know he did, dear. Look how he liked that photograph you gave him.

FRANK [*startled*]: What about it?

DORA: Nothing dear. Just that he pestered you to have it as soon as he saw it. Do you remember? [*To* DYSART.] We've always been a horsey family. At least my side of it has. My grandfather used to ride every morning on the downs behind Brighton, all dressed up in bowler hat and jodhpurs! He used to look splendid. Indulging in equitation, he called it.

[FRANK *moves away from them and sits wearily.*]

ALAN [*trying the word*]: Equitation . . .

DORA: I remember I told him how that came from *equus*, the Latin word for horse. Alan was fascinated by that word, I know. I suppose because he'd never come across one with two 'u's together before.

ALAN [*savouring it*]: *Equus!*

DORA: I always wanted the boy to ride himself. He'd have so enjoyed it.

DYSART: But surely he did?

DORA: No.

DYSART: Never?

DORA: He didn't care for it. He was most definite about not wanting to.

DYSART: But he must have had to at the stables? I mean, it would be part of the job.

DORA: You'd have thought so, but no. He absolutely wouldn't, would he, dear?

FRANK [*dryly*]: It seems he was perfectly happy raking out manure.

DYSART: Did he ever give a reason for this?

DORA: No. I must say we both thought it most peculiar, but he wouldn't discuss it. I mean, you'd have thought he'd be longing to get out in the air after being cooped up all week in that dreadful shop. Electrical and kitchenware! Isn't *that* an environment for a sensitive boy, Doctor? . . .

FRANK: Dear, have you offered the doctor a cup of tea?

DORA: Oh dear, no, I haven't! . . . And you must be dying for one.

DYSART: That would be nice.

DORA: Of course it would . . . Excuse me . . .

[*She goes out – but lingers on the circle, eavesdropping near the right door.* ALAN *stretches out under his blanket and sleeps.* FRANK *gets up.*]

FRANK: My wife has romantic ideas, if you receive my meaning.

DYSART: About her family?

FRANK: She thinks she married beneath her. I daresay she did. I don't understand these things myself.

DYSART: Mr Strang, I'm fascinated by the fact that Alan wouldn't ride.

FRANK: Yes, well that's him. He's always been a weird lad, I have to be honest. Can you imagine spending your week-ends like that – just cleaning out stalls – with all the things that he could have been doing in the way of Further Education?

DYSART: Except he's hardly a scholar.

FRANK: How do we know? He's never really tried. His mother indulged him. She doesn't care if he can hardly write his own name, and she a school teacher that was. Just as long as he's happy, she says . . .

[DORA *wrings her hands in anguish.*
FRANK *sits again.*]

DYSART: Would you say she was closer to him than you are?

FRANK: They've always been thick as thieves. I can't say I entirely approve – especially when I hear her whispering that Bible to him hour after hour, up there in his room.

DYSART: Your wife is religious?

FRANK: Some might say excessively so. Mind you, that's her business.

But when it comes to dosing it down the boy's throat – well, frankly, he's my son as well as hers. She doesn't see that. Of course, that's the funny thing about religious people. They always think their susceptibilities are more important than non-religious.

DYSART: And you're non-religious, I take it?

FRANK: I'm an atheist, and I don't mind admitting it. If you want my opinion, it's the Bible that's responsible for all this.

DYSART: Why?

FRANK: Well, look at it yourself. A boy spends night after night having this stuff read into him; an innocent man tortured to death – thorns driven into his head – nails into his hands – a spear jammed through his ribs. It can mark anyone for life, that kind of thing. I'm not joking. The boy was absolutely fascinated by all that. He was always mooning over religious pictures. I mean real kinky ones, if you receive my meaning. I had to put a stop to it once or twice! . . . [*Pause.*] Bloody religion – it's our only real problem in this house, but it's insuperable; I don't mind admitting it.

[*Unable to stand any more,* DORA *comes in again.*]

DORA [*pleasantly*]: You must excuse my husband, Doctor. This one subject is something of an obsession with him, isn't it, dear? You must admit.

FRANK: Call it what you like. All that stuff to me is just bad sex.

DORA: And what has that got to do with Alan?

FRANK: Everything! . . . [*Seriously.*] Everything, Dora!

DORA: I don't understand. What are you saying?

[*He turns away from her.*]

DYSART [*calmingly*]: Mr Strang, exactly how informed do you judge your son to *be* about sex?

FRANK [*tight*]: I don't know.

DYSART: You didn't actually instruct him yourself?

FRANK: Not in so many words, no.

DYSART: Did *you*, Mrs Strang?

DORA: Well, I spoke a little, yes. I had to. I've been a teacher, Doctor, and I know what happens if you don't. They find out through magazines and dirty books.

DYSART: What sort of thing did you tell him? I'm sorry if this is embarrassing.

DORA: I told him the biological facts. But I also told him what I believed. That sex is not *just* a biological matter, but spiritual as well. That if God willed, he would fall in love one day. That his task was to prepare himself for the most important happening of his life. And after that, if he was lucky, he might come to know a higher love still . . . I simply . . . don't understand . . . *Alan!* . . .

[*She breaks down in sobs.*

Her husband gets up and goes to her.]

FRANK [*embarrassed*]: There now. There now, Dora. Come on!

DORA [*with sudden desperation*]: All right – laugh! Laugh, as usual!

FRANK [*kindly*]: No one's laughing, Dora.

[*She glares at him. He puts his arms round her shoulders.*]

No one's laughing, are they Doctor?

[*Tenderly, he leads his wife out of the square, and they resume their places on the bench.*

Lights grow much dimmer.]

8

[*A strange noise begins.* ALAN *begins to murmur from his bed. He is having a bad nightmare, moving his hands and body as if frantically straining to tug something back.*

DYSART *leaves the square as the boy's cries increase.*]

ALAN: Ek! . . . Ek! . . . *Ek!* . . .

[*Cries of Ek! on tape fill the theatre, from all around.*

DYSART *reaches the foot of* ALAN's *bed as the boy gives a terrible cry –*

EK!

– and wakes up. The sounds snap off. ALAN *and the Doctor stare at each other. Then abruptly* DYSART *leaves the area and re-enters the square.*]

[*Lights grow brighter.*

DYSART *sits on his bench, left, and opens his file.* ALAN *gets out of bed, leaves his blanket, and comes in. He looks truculent.*]

DYSART: Hallo. How are you this morning?

[ALAN *stares at him.*]

Come on: sit down.

[ALAN *crosses the stage and sits on the bench, opposite.*]

Sorry if I gave you a start last night. I was collecting some papers from my office, and I thought I'd look in on you. Do you dream often?

ALAN: Do *you*?

DYSART: It's my job to ask the questions. Yours to answer them.

ALAN: Says who?

DYSART: Says me. Do you dream often?

ALAN: Do you?

DYSART: Look – Alan.

ALAN: I'll answer if you answer. In turns.

[*Pause.*]

DYSART: Very well. Only we have to speak the truth.

ALAN [*mocking*]: Very well.

DYSART: So. Do you dream often?

ALAN: Yes. Do you?

DYSART: Yes. Do you have a special dream?

ALAN: No. Do you?

DYSART: Yes. What was your dream about last night?

ALAN: Can't remember. What's yours about?

DYSART: I said the truth.

ALAN: That is the truth. What's yours about? The special one.

DYSART: Carving up children.

[ALAN *smiles.*]

My turn!

ALAN: What?

DYSART: What is your first memory of a horse?

ALAN: What d'you mean?

DYSART: The first time one entered your life, in any way.

ALAN: Can't remember.

DYSART: Are you sure?

ALAN: Yes.

DYSART: You have no recollection of the first time you noticed a horse?

ALAN: I told you. Now it's my turn. Are you married?

DYSART [controlling himself]: I am.

ALAN: Is she a doctor too?

DYSART: It's my turn.

ALAN: Yes, well what?

DYSART: What is Ek?

[Pause.]

You shouted it out last night in your sleep. I thought you might like to talk about it.

ALAN [singing]: Double Diamond works wonders,

Works wonders, works wonders!

DYSART: Come on, now. You can do better than that.

ALAN [singing louder]: Double Diamond works wonders,

Works wonders

For you!

DYSART: All right. Good morning.

ALAN: What d'you mean?

DYSART: We're finished for today.

ALAN: But I've only had ten minutes.

DYSART: Too bad.

[He picks up a file and studies it.

ALAN lingers.]

Didn't you hear me? I said, Good morning.

ALAN: That's not fair!

DYSART: No?

ALAN [savagely]: The Government pays you twenty quid an hour to see me. I know. I heard downstairs.

DYSART: Well, go back there and hear some more.

ALAN: *That's not fair!*

[*He springs up, clenching his fists in a sudden violent rage.*]

You're a – you're a – You're a swiz! ... Bloody swiz! ... Fucking swiz!

DYSART: Do I have to call Nurse?

ALAN: She puts a finger on me, I'll bash her!

DYSART: She'll bash you much harder, I can assure you. Now go away.

[*He reads his file.* ALAN *stays where he is, emptily clenching his hands. He turns away.*

A pause.

A faint hum starts from the CHORUS.]

ALAN [*sullenly*]: On a beach ...

10

[*He steps out of the square, upstage, and begins to walk round the circle. Warm light glows on it.*]

DYSART: What?

ALAN: Where I saw a horse. Swizzy.

[*Lazily he kicks at the sand, and throws stones at the sea.*]

DYSART: How old were you?

ALAN: How should I know? ... Six.

DYSART: Well, go on. What were you doing there?

ALAN: Digging.

[*He throws himself on the ground, downstage centre of the circle, and starts scuffing with his hands.*]

DYSART: A sandcastle?

ALAN: Well, what else?

DYSART [*warningly*]: And?

ALAN: Suddenly I heard this noise. Coming up behind me.

[*A young* HORSEMAN *issues in* slow motion *out of the tunnel. He*

*carries a riding crop with which he is urging on his invisible horse,
down the right side of the circle.*

The hum increases.]

DYSART: What noise?

ALAN: Hooves. Splashing.

DYSART: Splashing?

ALAN: The tide was out and he was galloping.

DYSART: Who was?

ALAN: This fellow. Like a college chap. He was on a big horse –
urging him on. I thought he hadn't seen me. I called out: Hey!

[*The* HORSEMAN *goes into* natural time, *charging fast round the
downstage corner of the square straight at* ALAN.]

and they just swerved in time!

HORSEMAN [*reining back*]: Whoa! ... Whoa there! *Whoa!* ...
Sorry! I didn't see you! ... Did I scare you?

ALAN: No!

HORSEMAN [*looking down on him*]: That's a terrific castle!

ALAN: What's his name?

HORSEMAN: Trojan. You can stroke him, if you like. He won't
mind.

[*Shyly* ALAN *stretches up on tip-toe, and pats an invisible shoulder.*
[*Amused.*] You can hardly reach down there. Would you like to
come up?

[ALAN *nods, eyes wide.*]

All right. Come round this side. You always mount a horse from
the left. I'll give you a lift. O.K.?

[ALAN *goes round on the other side.*]

Here we go, now. Just do nothing. Upsadaisy!

[ALAN *sets his foot on the* HORSEMAN'S *thigh, and is lifted by him up
on to his shoulders.*

The hum from the CHORUS *becomes exultant. Then stops.*]

All right?

[ALAN *nods.*]

Good. Now all you do is hold onto his mane.

[*He holds up the crop, and* ALAN *grips on to it.*]

Tight now. And grip with your knees. All right?

All set? . . . Come on, then, Trojan. Let's go!

[*The* HORSEMAN *walks slowly upstage round the circle, with* ALAN's *legs tight round his neck.*]

DYSART: How was it? Was it wonderful?

[ALAN *rides in silence.*]

Can't you remember?

HORSEMAN: Do you want to go faster?

ALAN: Yes!

HORSEMAN: O.K. All you have to do is say 'Come on, Trojan – bear me away!' . . . Say it, then!

ALAN: Bear me away!

[*The* HORSEMAN *starts to run with* ALAN *round the circle.*]

DYSART: You went fast?

ALAN: Yes!

DYSART: Weren't you frightened?

ALAN: No!

HORSEMAN: Come on now, Trojan! Bear us away! Hold on! Come on now! . . .

[*He runs faster.* ALAN *begins to laugh. Then suddenly, as they reach again the right downstage corner,* FRANK *and* DORA *stand up in alarm.*]

DORA: Alan!

FRANK: Alan!

DORA: Alan, stop!

[FRANK *runs round after them.* DORA *follows behind.*]

FRANK: Hey, you! *You!* . . .

HORSEMAN: Whoa, boy! . . . Whoa! . . .

[*He reins the horse round, and wheels to face the parents. This all goes fast.*]

FRANK: What do you imagine you are doing?

HORSEMAN [*ironic*]: 'Imagine?'

FRANK: What is my son doing up there?

HORSEMAN: Water-skiing!

[DORA *joins them, breathless.*]

DORA: Is he all right, Frank? . . . He's not hurt?

FRANK: Don't you think you should ask permission before doing a stupid thing like that?

HORSEMAN: What's stupid?

ALAN: It's lovely, dad!

DORA: Alan, come down here!

HORSEMAN: The boy's perfectly safe. Please don't be hysterical.

FRANK: Don't you be la-di-da with me, young man! Come down here, Alan. You heard what your mother said.

ALAN: No.

FRANK: Come down at once. Right this moment.

ALAN: No . . . NO!

FRANK [*in a fury*]: I said – this moment!

[*He pulls* ALAN *from the horseman's shoulders. The boy shrieks, and falls to the ground.*]

HORSEMAN: Watch it!

DORA: Frank!

[*She runs to her son, and kneels. The* HORSEMAN *skitters.*]

HORSEMAN: Are you mad? D'you want to terrify the horse?

DORA: He's grazed his knee. Frank – the boy's hurt!

ALAN: I'm not! I'm *not*!

FRANK: What's your name?

HORSEMAN: Jesse James.

DORA: Frank, he's bleeding!

FRANK: I intend to report you to the police for endangering the lives of children.

HORSEMAN: Go right ahead!

DORA: Can you stand, dear?

ALAN: Oh, *stop* it! . . .

FRANK: You're a public menace, d'you know that? How dare you pick up children and put them on dangerous animals.

HORSEMAN: Dangerous?

FRANK: Of course dangerous. Look at his eyes. They're rolling.

HORSEMAN: So are yours!

FRANK: In my opinion that is a dangerous animal. In my considered opinion you are both dangers to the safety of this beach.

HORSEMAN: And in my opinion, you're a stupid fart!

DORA: Frank, leave it!

FRANK: What did you say?

DORA: It's not important, Frank – really!

FRANK: *What did you say?*

HORSEMAN: Oh bugger off! Sorry, chum! Come on, Trojan!

[*He urges his horse straight at them, then wheels it and gallops off round the right side of the circle and away up the tunnel, out of sight. The parents cry out, as they are covered with sand and water.* FRANK *runs after him, and round the left side of the circle, with his wife following after.*]

ALAN: Splash, splash, splash! All three of us got covered with water! Dad got absolutely soaked!

FRANK [*shouting after the* HORSEMAN]: Hooligan! Filthy hooligan!

ALAN: I wanted to laugh!

FRANK: Upper-class riff-raff! That's all they are, people who go riding! That's what they *want* – trample on ordinary people!

DORA: Don't be absurd, Frank.

FRANK: It's why they do it. It's why they bloody do it!

DORA [*amused*]: Look at you. You're covered!

FRANK: Not as much as you. There's sand all over your hair!

[*She starts to laugh.*]

[*Shouting.*] Hooligan! Bloody hooligan!

[*She starts to laugh more. He tries to brush the sand out of her hair.*]

What are you laughing at? It's not funny. It's not funny at all. Dora!

[*She goes off, right, still laughing.* ALAN *edges into the square, still on the ground.*]

It's just not funny! . . .

[FRANK *returns to his place on the beach, sulky. Abrupt silence.*]

ALAN: And that's all I remember.

DYSART: And a lot, too. Thank you . . . You know, I've never been on a horse in my life.

ALAN [*not looking at him*]: Nor me.

DYSART: You mean, after that?

ALAN: Yes.

DYSART: But you must have done at the stables?

ALAN: No.

DYSART: Never?

ALAN: No.

DYSART: How come?

ALAN: I didn't care to.

DYSART: Did it have anything to do with falling off like that, all those years ago?

ALAN [*tight*]: I just didn't care to, that's all.

DYSART: Do you think of that scene often?

ALAN: I suppose.

DYSART: Why, do you think?

ALAN: 'Cos it's funny.

DYSART: Is that all?

ALAN: What else? My turn . . . I told you a secret; now you tell me one.

DYSART: All right. I have patients who've got things to tell me, only they're ashamed to say them to my face. What do you think I do about that?

ALAN: What?

DYSART: I give them this little tape recorder.

[*He takes a small tape recorder and microphone from his pocket.*]

They go off to another room, and send me the tape through Nurse. They don't have to listen to it with me.

ALAN: That's stupid.

DYSART: All you do is press this button, and speak into this. It's very simple. Anyway, your time's up for today. I'll see you tomorrow.

ALAN [*getting up*]: Maybe.

DYSART: Maybe?

ALAN: If I feel like it.

[*He is about to go out. Then suddenly he returns to* DYSART *and takes the machine from him.*]

It's stupid.

[*He leaves the square and goes back to his bed.*]

11

DORA [*calling out*]: Doctor!

[*DORA re-enters and comes straight on to the square from the right. She wears an overcoat, and is nervously carrying a shopping bag.*]

DYSART: That same evening, his mother appeared.

DORA: Hallo, Doctor.

DYSART: Mrs Strang!

DORA: I've been shopping in the neighbourhood. I thought I might just look in.

DYSART: Did you want to see Alan?

DORA [*uncomfortably*]: No, no . . . Not just at the moment. Actually, it's more you I wanted to see.

DYSART: Yes?

DORA: You see, there's something Mr Strang and I thought you ought to know. We discussed it, and it might just be important.

DYSART: Well, come and sit down.

DORA: I can't stay more than a moment. I'm late as it is. Mr Strang will be wanting his dinner.

DYSART: Ah. [*Encouragingly.*] So, what was it you wanted to tell me?

[*She sits on the upstage bench.*]

DORA: Well, do you remember that photograph I mentioned to you. The one Mr Strang gave Alan to decorate his bedroom a few years ago?

DYSART: Yes. A horse looking over a gate, wasn't it?

DORA: That's right. Well, actually, it took the place of another kind of picture altogether.

DYSART: What kind?

DORA: It was a reproduction of Our Lord on his way to Calvary. Alan found it in Reeds Art Shop, and fell absolutely in love with it. He insisted on buying it with his pocket money, and hanging it at the foot of his bed where he could see it last thing at night. My husband was very displeased.

44

DYSART: Because it was religious?

DORA: In all fairness I must admit it was a little extreme. The Christ was loaded down with chains, and the centurions were really laying on the stripes. It certainly would not have been my choice, but I don't believe in interfering too much with children, so I said nothing.

DYSART: But Mr Strang did?

DORA: He stood it for a while, but one day we had one of our tiffs about religion, and he went upstairs, tore it off the boy's wall and threw it in the dustbin. Alan went quite hysterical. He cried for days without stopping – and he was not a crier, you know.

DYSART: But he recovered when he was given the photograph of the horse in its place?

DORA: He certainly seemed to. At least, he hung it in exactly the same position, and we had no more of that awful weeping.

DYSART: Thank you, Mrs Strang. That *is* interesting ... Exactly how long ago was that? Can you remember?

DORA: It must be five years ago, Doctor. Alan would have been about twelve. How is he, by the way?

DYSART: Bearing up.

[*She rises.*]

DORA: Please give him my love.

DYSART: You can see him any time you want, you know.

DORA: Perhaps if I could come one afternoon without Mr Strang. He and Alan don't exactly get on at the moment, as you can imagine.

DYSART. Whatever you decide, Mrs Strang ... Oh, one thing.

DORA: Yes?

DYSART: Could you describe that photograph of the horse in a little more detail for me? I presume it's still in his bedroom?

DORA: Oh, yes. It's a most remarkable picture, really. You very rarely see a horse taken from that angle – absolutely head on. That's what makes it so interesting.

DYSART: Why? What does it look like?

DORA: Well, it's most extraordinary. It comes out all eyes.

DYSART: Staring straight at you?

DORA: Yes, that's right . . .

[*An uncomfortable pause.*]

I'll come and see him one day very soon, Doctor. Goodbye.

[*She leaves, and resumes her place by her husband.*]

DYSART [*to audience*]: It was then – that moment – I felt real alarm. What was it? The shadow of a giant head across my desk? . . . At any rate, the feeling got worse with the stable-owner's visit.

12

[DALTON *comes in to the square: heavy-set, mid-fifties.*]

DALTON: Dr Dysart?

DYSART: Mr Dalton. It's very good of you to come.

DALTON: It is, actually. In my opinion the boy should be in prison. Not in a hospital at the tax-payers' expense.

DYSART: Please sit down.

[DALTON *sits.*]

This must have been a terrible experience for you.

DALTON: Terrible? I don't think I'll ever get over it. Jill's had a nervous breakdown.

DYSART: Jill?

DALTON: The girl who worked for me. Of course, she feels responsible in a way. Being the one who introduced him in the first place.

DYSART: He was introduced to the stable by a girl?

DALTON: Jill Mason. He met her somewhere, and asked for a job. She told him to come and see me. I wish to Christ she never had.

DYSART: But when he first appeared he didn't seem in any way peculiar?

DALTON: No, he was bloody good. He'd spend hours with the horses cleaning and grooming them, way over the call of duty. I thought he was a real find.

DYSART: Apparently, during the whole time he worked for you, he never actually rode.

DALTON: That's true.

DYSART: Wasn't that peculiar?

DALTON: Very ... *If* he didn't.

DYSART: What do you mean?

[DALTON *rises.*]

DALTON: Because on and off, that whole year, I had the feeling the horses were being taken out at night.

DYSART: At night?

DALTON: There were just odd things I noticed. I mean too often one or other of them would be sweaty first thing in the morning, when it wasn't sick. Very sweaty, too. And its stall wouldn't be near as mucky as it should be if it had been in all night. I never paid it much mind at the time. It was only when I realized I'd been hiring a loony, I came to wonder if he hadn't been riding all the time, behind our backs.

DYSART: But wouldn't you have noticed if things had been disturbed?

DALTON: Nothing ever was. Still, he's a neat worker. That wouldn't prove anything.

DYSART: Aren't the stables locked at night?

DALTON: Yes.

DYSART: And someone sleeps on the premises?

DALTON: Me and my son.

DYSART: Two people?

DALTON: I'm sorry, Doctor. It's obviously just my fancy. I tell you, this thing has shaken me so bad, I'm liable to believe anything. If there's nothing else, I'll be going.

DYSART: Look: even if you were right, why should anyone do that? Why would any boy prefer to ride by himself at night, when he could go off with others during the day?

DALTON: Are you asking me? He's a loony, isn't he?

[DALTON *leaves the square and sits again in his place.* DYSART *watches him go.*]

ALAN: It was *sexy.*

DYSART: His tape arrived that evening.

[ALAN *is sitting on his bed holding the tape recorder.* NURSE *approaches briskly, takes the machine from him – gives it to* DYSART *in the square – and leaves again, resuming her seat.* DYSART *switches on the tape.*]

ALAN: That's what you want to know, isn't it? All right: it was. I'm talking about the beach. That time when I was a kid. What I told you about . . .

[*Pause. He is in great emotional difficulty.*

DYSART *sits on the left bench listening, file in hand.* ALAN *rises and stands directly behind him, but on the circle, as if recording the ensuing speech. He never, of course, looks directly at the Doctor.*]

I was pushed forward on the horse. There was sweat on my legs from his neck. The fellow held me tight, and let me turn the horse which way I wanted. All that power going any way you wanted . . . His sides were all warm, and the smell . . . Then suddenly I was on the ground, where Dad pulled me. I could have bashed him . . .

[*Pause.*]

Something else. When the horse first appeared, I looked up into his mouth. It was huge. There was this chain in it. The fellow pulled it, and cream dripped out. I said 'Does it hurt?' And he said – the horse said – said –

[*He stops, in anguish.* DYSART *makes a note in his file.*]

[*Desperately.*] It was always the same, after that. Every time I heard one clop by, I had to run and see. Up a country lane or anywhere. They sort of pulled me. I couldn't take my eyes off them. Just to watch their skins. The way their necks twist, and sweat shines in the folds . . . [*Pause.*] I can't remember when it started. Mum reading to me about Prince who no one could ride, except one boy. Or the white horse in Revelations. 'He that sat upon him was called Faithful and True. His eyes were as flames of fire, and he had a name written that no man knew but himself' . . . Words like reins Stirrup. Flanks . . . 'Dashing his spurs against his charger's flanks!'

... Even the words made me feel – Years, I never told anyone. Mum wouldn't understand. She likes 'Equitation'. Bowler hats and jodhpurs! 'My grandfather dressed for the horse,' she says. What does that mean? The horse isn't dressed. It's the most naked thing you ever saw! More than a dog or a cat or anything. Even the most broken down old nag has got its *life*! To put a bowler on it is *filthy*! ... Putting them through their paces! Bloody gymkhanas! ... No one understands! ... Except cowboys. They do. I wish I was a cowboy. They're free. They just swing up and then it's miles of grass ... I bet all cowboys are *orphans*! ... I bet they are!

NURSE: Mr Strang to see you, Doctor.

DYSART [*in surprise*]: Mr Strang? Show him up, please.

ALAN: No one ever says to cowboys 'Receive my meaning'! They wouldn't dare. Or 'God' all the time. [*Mimicking his mother.*] 'God sees you, Alan. God's got eyes everywhere –'

[*He stops abruptly.*]

I'm not doing any more! ... I hate this! ... You can whistle for any more. I've had it!

[*He returns angrily to his bed, throwing the blanket over him.* DYSART *switches off the tape.*]

14

[FRANK STRANG *comes into the square, his hat in his hand. He is nervous and embarrassed.*]

DYSART [*welcoming*]: Hallo, Mr Strang.

FRANK: I was just passing. I hope it's not too late.

DYSART: Of course not. I'm delighted to see you.

FRANK: My wife doesn't know I'm here. I'd be grateful to you if you didn't enlighten her, if you receive my meaning.

DYSART: Everything that happens in this room is confidential, Mr Strang.

FRANK: I hope so ... I hope so ...

DYSART [*gently*]: Do you have something to tell me?

FRANK: As a matter of fact I have. Yes.

DYSART: Your wife told me about the photograph.

FRANK: I know, it's not that! It's *about* that, but it's – worse ... I wanted to tell you the other night, but I couldn't in front of Dora. Maybe I should have. It might show her where all that stuff leads to, she drills into the boy behind my back.

DYSART: What kind of thing is it?

FRANK: Something I witnessed.

DYSART: Where?

FRANK: At home. About eighteen months ago.

DYSART: Go on.

FRANK: It was late. I'd gone upstairs to fetch something. The boy had been in bed hours, or so I thought.

DYSART: Go on.

FRANK: As I came along the passage I saw the door of his bedroom was ajar. I'm sure he didn't know it was. From inside I heard the sound of this chanting.

DYSART: Chanting?

FRANK: Like the Bible. One of those lists his mother's always reading to him.

DYSART: What kind of list?

FRANK: Those Begats. So-and-so begat, you know. Genealogy.

DYSART: Can you remember what Alan's list sounded like?

FRANK: Well, the *sort* of thing. I stood there absolutely astonished. The first word I heard was ...

ALAN [*rising and chanting*]: Prince!

DYSART: Prince?

FRANK: Prince begat Prince. That sort of nonsense.

[ALAN *moves slowly to the centre of the circle, downstage.*]

ALAN: And Prance begat Prankus! And Prankus begat Flankus!

FRANK: I looked through the door, and he was standing in the moonlight in his pyjamas, right in front of that big photograph.

DYSART: The horse with the huge eyes?

FRANK: Right.

ALAN: Flankus begat Spankus. And Spankus begat Spunkus the Great, who lived three score years!

FRANK: It was all like that. I can't remember the exact names, of course. Then suddenly he knelt down.

DYSART: In front of the photograph?

FRANK: Yes. Right there at the foot of his bed.

ALAN [*kneeling*]: And Legwus begat Neckwus. And Neckwus begat Fleckwus, the King of Spit. And Fleckwus spoke out of his chinkle-chankle!

[*He bows himself to the ground.*]

DYSART: What?

FRANK: I'm sure that was the word. I've never forgotten it. Chinkle-chankle.

[ALAN *raises his head and extends his hands up in glory.*]

ALAN: And he said 'Behold – I give you Equus, my only begotten son!'

DYSART: Equus?

FRANK: Yes. No doubt of that. He repeated that word several times. 'Equus my only begotten son.'

ALAN [*reverently*]: Ek ... wus!

DYSART [*suddenly understanding: almost 'aside'*]: Ek ... Ek ...

FRANK [*embarrassed*]: And then ...

DYSART: Yes: what?

FRANK: He took a piece of string out of his pocket. Made up into a noose. And put it in his mouth.

[ALAN *bridles himself with invisible string, and pulls it back.*]

And then with his other hand he picked up a coat hanger. A wooden coat hanger, and – and –

DYSART: Began to beat himself?

[ALAN, *in mime, begins to thrash himself, increasing the strokes in speed and viciousness.*

Pause.]

FRANK: You see why I couldn't tell his mother ... Religion. Religion's at the bottom of all this!

DYSART: What did you do?

FRANK: Nothing. I coughed – and went back downstairs.

[*The boy starts guiltily – tears the string from his mouth – and scrambles back to bed.*]

DYSART: Did you ever speak to him about it later? Even obliquely?

FRANK [*unhappily*]: I can't speak of things like that, Doctor. It's not in my nature.

DYSART [*kindly*]: No. I see that.

FRANK: But I thought you ought to know. So I came.

DYSART [*warmly*]: Yes. I'm very grateful to you. Thank you.

[*Pause.*]

FRANK: Well, that's it . . .

DYSART: Is there anything else?

FRANK [*even more embarrassed*]: There is actually. One thing.

DYSART: What's that?

FRANK: On the night that he did it – that awful thing in the stable –

DYSART: Yes?

FRANK: That very night, he was out with a girl.

DYSART: How d'you know that?

FRANK: I just know.

DYSART [*puzzled*]: Did he tell you?

FRANK: I can't say any more.

DYSART: I don't quite understand.

FRANK: Everything said in here is confidential, you said.

DYSART: Absolutely.

FRANK: Then ask him. Ask him about taking a girl out, that very night he did it . . . [*Abruptly.*] Goodbye, Doctor.

[*He goes.* DYSART *looks after him.*

FRANK *resumes his seat.*]

15

[ALAN *gets up and enters the square.*]

DYSART: Alan! Come in. Sit down. [*Pleasantly.*] What did you do last night?

ALAN: Watched telly.

DYSART: Any good?

ALAN: All right.

DYSART: Thanks for the tape. It was excellent.

ALAN: I'm not making any more.

DYSART: One thing I didn't quite understand. You began to say something about the horse on the beach talking to you.

ALAN: That's stupid. Horses don't talk.

DYSART: So I believe.

ALAN: I don't know what you mean.

DYSART: Never mind. Tell me something else. Who introduced you to the stable to begin with?

[Pause.]

ALAN: Someone I met.

DYSART: Where?

ALAN: Bryson's.

DYSART: The shop where you worked?

ALAN: Yes.

DYSART: That's a funny place for you to be. Whose idea was that?

ALAN: Dad.

DYSART: I'd have thought he'd have wanted you to work with him.

ALAN: I haven't the aptitude. And printing's a failing trade. If you receive my meaning.

DYSART [amused]: I see . . . What did your mother think?

ALAN: Shops are common.

DYSART: And you?

ALAN: I loved it.

DYSART: Really?

ALAN [sarcastic]: Why not? You get to spend every minute with electrical things. It's fun.

[NURSE, DALTON and the actors playing horses call out to him as CUSTOMERS, seated where they are. Their voices are aggressive and demanding. There is a constant background mumbling, made up of trade names, out of which can clearly be distinguished the italicized words, which are shouted out.]

53

CUSTOMER: *Philco!*

ALAN [*to* DYSART]: Of course it might just drive you off your chump.

CUSTOMER: I want to buy a hot-plate. I'm told the *Philco* is a good make!

ALAN: I think it is, madam.

CUSTOMER: *Remington* ladies' shavers?

ALAN: I'm not sure, madam.

CUSTOMER: *Robex* tableware?

CUSTOMER: *Croydex?*

CUSTOMER: *Volex?*

CUSTOMER: *Pifco* automatic toothbrushes?

ALAN: I'll find out, sir.

CUSTOMER: Beautiflor!

CUSTOMER: Windowlene!

CUSTOMER: I want a *Philco* transistor radio!

CUSTOMER: This isn't a *Remington!* I wanted a *Remington!*

ALAN: Sorry.

CUSTOMER: Are you a dealer for *Hoover?*

ALAN: Sorry.

CUSTOMER: I wanted the heat-retaining *Pifco!*

ALAN: *Sorry!*

> [*JILL comes into the square; a girl in her early twenties, pretty and middle class. She wears a sweater and jeans. The mumbling stops.*]

JILL: Hallo.

ALAN: Hallo.

JILL: Have you any blades for a clipping machine?

ALAN: Clipping?

JILL: To clip horses.

> [*Pause. He stares at her, open-mouthed.*]

What's the matter?

ALAN: You work at Dalton's stables. I've seen you.

> [*During the following, he mimes putting away a pile of boxes on a shelf in the shop.*]

JILL: I've seen you too, haven't I? You're the boy who's always staring into the yard around lunch-time.

ALAN: Me?

JILL: You're there most days.

ALAN: Not me.

JILL [amused]: Of course it's you. Mr Dalton was only saying the other day: 'Who's that boy keeps staring in at the door?' Are you looking for a job or something?

ALAN [eagerly]: Is there one?

JILL: I don't know.

ALAN: I can only do week-ends.

JILL: That's when most people ride. We can always use extra hands. It'd mainly be mucking out.

ALAN: I don't mind.

JILL: Can you ride?

ALAN: No . . . No . . . I don't want to.

[She looks at him curiously.]

Please.

JILL: Come up on Saturday. I'll introduce you to Mr Dalton.

[She leaves the square.]

DYSART: When was this? About a year ago?

ALAN: I suppose.

DYSART: And she did?

ALAN: Yes.

[Briskly he moves the three benches to form three stalls in the stable.]

16

[Rich light falls on the square.
An exultant humming from the CHORUS.
Tramping is heard. Three actors playing horses rise from their places.
Together they unhook three horse masks from the ladders to left and
right, put them on with rigid timing, and walk with swaying horse-
motion into the square. Their metal hooves stamp on the wood. Their
masks turn and toss high above their heads – as they will do sporadically
throughout all horse scenes – making the steel gleam in the light.

For a moment they seem to converge on the boy as he stands in the middle of the stable, but then they swiftly turn and take up positions as if tethered by the head, with their invisible rumps towards him, one by each bench.

ALAN is sunk in this glowing world of horses. Lost in wonder, he starts almost involuntarily to kneel on the floor in reverence – but is sharply interrupted by the cheery voice of DALTON, coming into the stable, followed by JILL. The boy straightens up guiltily.]

DALTON: First thing to learn is drill. Learn it and keep to it. I want this place neat, dry and clean at all times. After you've mucked out, Jill will show you some grooming. What we call strapping a horse.

JILL: I think Trooper's got a stone.

DALTON: Yes? Let's see.

[He crosses to the horse by the left bench, who is balancing one hoof on its tip. He picks up the hoof.]

You're right. [*To* ALAN.] See this? This V here. It's what's called a frog. Sort of shock-absorber. Once you pierce that, it takes ages to heal – so you want to watch for it. You clean it out with this. What we call a hoof-pick.

[He takes from his pocket an invisible pick.]

Mind how you go with it. It's very sharp. Use it like this.

[He quickly takes the stone out.]

See?

[ALAN nods, fascinated.]

You'll soon get the hang of it. Jill will look after you. What she doesn't know about stables, isn't worth knowing.

JILL [*pleased*]: Oh yes, I'm sure!

DALTON [*handing* ALAN *the pick*]: Careful how you go with that. The main rule i s, anything you don't know: ask. Never pretend you know something when you don't. [*Smiling.*] Actually, the main rule is: enjoy yourself. All right?

ALAN: Yes, sir.

DALTON: Good lad. See you later.

[He nods to them cheerfully, and leaves the square. ALAN clearly puts the invisible hoof-pick on the rail, downstage left.]

JILL: All right, let's start on some grooming. Why don't we begin with him? He looks as if he needs it.

[*They approach* NUGGET, *who is standing to the right. She pats him.* ALAN *sits and watches her.*]

This is Nugget. He's my favourite. He's as gentle as a baby, aren't you? But terribly fast if you want him to be.

[*During the following, she mimes both the actions and the objects, which she picks up from the right bench.*]

Now this is the dandy, and we start with that. Then you move on to the body brush. This is the most important, and you use it with this curry-comb. Now you always groom the same way: from the ears downward. Don't be afraid to do it hard. The harder you do it, the more the horse loves it. Push it right through the coat: like this.

[*The boy watches in fascination as she brushes the invisible body of* NUGGET, *scraping the dirt and hair off on to the invisible curry-comb. Now and then the horse mask moves very slightly in pleasure.*]

Down towards the tail and right through the coat. See how he loves it? I'm giving you a lovely massage, boy, aren't I?... You try.

[*She hands him the brush. Gingerly he rises and approaches* NUGGET. *Embarrassed and excited, he copies her movements, inexpertly.*]

Keep it nice and easy. Never rush. Down towards the tail and right through the coat. That's it. Again. Down towards the tail and right through the coat... Very good. Now you keep that up for fifteen minutes and then do old Trooper. Will you?

[ALAN *nods.*]

You've got a feel for it. I can tell. It's going to be nice teaching you. See you later.

[*She leaves the square and resumes her place.*
ALAN *is left alone with the horses.*
They all stamp. He approaches NUGGET *again, and touches the horse's shoulder. The mask turns sharply in his direction. The boy pauses, then moves his hand gently over the outline of the neck and back. The mask is reassured. It stares ahead unmoving. Then* ALAN *lifts his palm to his face and smells it deeply, closing his eyes.*]

DYSART *rises from his bench, and begins to walk slowly upstage round the circle.*]

DYSART: Was that good? Touching them.

[ALAN *gives a faint groan.*]

ALAN: Mmm.

DYSART: It must have been marvellous, being near them at last . . . Stroking them . . . Making them fresh and glossy . . . Tell me . . .

[*Silence.* ALAN *begins to brush* NUGGET]

How about the girl? Did you like her?

ALAN [*tight*]: All right.

DYSART: Just all right?

[ALAN *changes his position, moving round* NUGGET'S *rump so that his back is to the audience. He brushes harder.* DYSART *comes downstage around the circle, and finally back to his bench.*]

Was she friendly?

ALAN: Yes.

DYSART: Or stand-offish?

ALAN: Yes.

DYSART: Well which?

ALAN: What?

DYSART: Which was she?

[ALAN *brushes harder.*]

Did you take her? Come on now: tell me. Did you have a date with her?

ALAN: What?

DYSART [*sitting*]: Tell me if you did.

[*The boy suddenly explodes in one of his rages.*]

ALAN [*yelling*]: TELL ME!

[*All the masks toss at the noise.*]

DYSART: What?

ALAN: *Tell me, tell me, tell me, tell me!*

[ALAN *storms out of the square, and downstage to where* DYSART *sits. He is raging. During the ensuing, the horses leave by all three openings.*]

On and on, sitting there! Nosey Parker! That's all you are! Bloody
Nosey Parker! Just like Dad. On and on and bloody on! Tell me,
tell me, tell me! ... Answer this. Answer that. Never stop! –

[*He marches round the circle and back into the square.* DYSART *rises
and enters it from the other side.*]

17

[*Lights brighten.*]

DYSART: I'm sorry.

[ALAN *slams about what is now the office again, replacing the benches
to their usual position.*]

ALAN: All right, it's my turn now. You tell me! Answer me!

DYSART: We're not playing that game now.

ALAN: We're playing what I say.

DYSART: All right. What do you want to know?

[*He sits.*]

ALAN: Do *you* have dates?

DYSART: I told you. I'm married.

[ALAN *approaches him, very hostile.*]

ALAN: I know. Her name's Margaret. She's a dentist! You see, I
found out! What made you go with her? Did you use to bite her
hands when she did you in the chair?

[*The boy sits next to him, close.*]

DYSART: That's not very funny.

ALAN: Do you have girls behind her back?

DYSART: No.

ALAN: Then what? Do you fuck her?

DYSART: That's enough now.

[*He rises and moves away.*]

ALAN: Come on, tell me! Tell me, tell me!

DYSART: I said that's enough now.

[ALAN *rises too and walks around him.*]

I bet you don't. I bet you never touch her. Come on, tell me. You've got no kids, have you? Is that because you don't fuck?

DYSART [*sharp*]: Go to your room. Go on: quick march.

[*Pause.* ALAN *moves away from him, insolently takes up a packet of* DYSART'*s cigarettes from the bench, and extracts one.*]

Give me those cigarettes.

[*The boy puts one in his mouth.*]

[*Exploding.*] Alan, *give them to me!*

[*Reluctantly* ALAN *shoves the cigarette back in the packet, turns and hands it to him.*]

Now go!

[ALAN *bolts out of the square, and back to his bed.* DYSART, *unnerved, addresses the audience.*]

Brilliant! Absolutely brilliant! The boy's on the run, so he gets defensive. What am *I*, then? . . . Wicked little bastard – he knew exactly what questions to try. He'd actually marched himself round the hospital, making inquiries about my wife. Wicked and – of course, perceptive. Ever since I made that crack about carving up children, he's been aware of me in an absolutely specific way. Of course, there's nothing novel in that. Advanced neurotics can be dazzling at that game. They aim unswervingly at your area of maximum vulnerability . . . Which I suppose is as good a way as any of describing Margaret.

[*He sits.* HESTHER *enters the square.*

Light grows warmer.]

18

HESTHER: Now stop it.

DYSART: Do I embarrass you?

HESTHER: I suspect you're about to.

[*Pause.*]

DYSART: My wife doesn't understand me, Your Honour.

HESTHER: Do you understand her?

DYSART: No. Obviously I never did.

HESTHER: I'm sorry. I've never liked to ask but I've always imagined you weren't exactly compatible.

[*She moves to sit opposite.*]

DYSART: We were. It actually worked for a bit. I mean for both of us. We worked for each other. She actually for me through a kind of briskness. A clear, red-headed, inaccessible briskness which kept me keyed up for months. Mind you, if you're kinky for Northern Hygienic, as I am, you can't find anything much more compelling than a Scottish Lady Dentist.

HESTHER: It's *you* who are wicked, you know!

DYSART: Not at all. She got exactly the same from me. Antiseptic proficiency. I was like that in those days. We suited each other admirably. I see us in our wedding photo: Doctor and Doctor Mac Brisk. We were brisk in our wooing, brisk in our wedding, brisk in our disappointment. We turned from each other briskly into our separate surgeries; and now there's damn all.

HESTHER: You have no children, have you?

DYSART: No, we didn't go in for them. Instead, she sits beside our salmon-pink, glazed brick fireplace, and knits things for orphans in a home she helps with. And I sit opposite, turning the pages of art books on Ancient Greece. Occasionally, I still trail a faint scent of my enthusiasm across her path. I pass her a picture of the sacred acrobats of Crete leaping through the horns of running bulls – and she'll say: 'Och, Martin, what an *absurred* thing to be doing! The Highland Games, now there's *norrmal* sport!' Or she'll observe, just after I've told her a story from the Iliad: 'You know, when you come to think of it, Agamemnon and that lot were nothing but a bunch of ruffians from the Gorbals, only with fancy names!' [*He rises.*] You get the picture. She's turned into a Shrink. The familiar domestic monster. Margaret Dysart: the Shrink's Shrink.

HESTHER: That's cruel, Martin.

DYSART: Yes. Do you know what it's like for two people to live in the same house as if they were in different parts of the world? Mentally, she's always in some drizzly kirk of her own inheriting:

and I'm in some Doric temple – clouds tearing through pillars – eagles bearing prophecies out of the sky. She finds all that repulsive. All my wife has ever taken from the Mediterranean – from that whole vast intuitive culture – are four bottles of Chianti to make into lamps, and two china condiment donkeys labelled Sally and Peppy.

[*Pause.*]

[*More intimately.*] I wish there was one person in my life I could show. One instinctive, absolutely unbrisk person I could take to Greece, and stand in front of certain shrines and sacred streams and say 'Look! Life is only comprehensible through a thousand local Gods. And not just the old dead ones with names like Zeus – no, but living Geniuses of Place and Person! And not just Greece but modern England! Spirits of certain trees, certain curves of brick wall, certain chip shops, if you like, and slate roofs – just as of certain frowns in people and slouches' . . . I'd say to them – 'Worship as many as you can see – and more will appear!' . . . If I had a son, I bet you he'd come out exactly like his mother. Utterly worshipless. Would you like a drink?

HESTHER: No, thanks. Actually, I've got to be going. As usual . . .

DYSART: Really?

HESTHER: Really. I've got an Everest of papers to get through before bed.

DYSART: You never stop, do you?

HESTHER: Do you?

DYSART: This boy, with his stare. He's trying to save himself through me.

HESTHER: I'd say so.

DYSART: What am I trying to do to him?

HESTHER: Restore him, surely?

DYSART: To what?

HESTHER: A normal life.

DYSART: Normal?

HESTHER: It still means something.

DYSART: Does it?

HESTHER: Of course.

DYSART: You mean a normal boy has one head: a normal head has two ears?

HESTHER: You know I don't.

DYSART: Then what else?

HESTHER [*lightly*]: Oh, stop it.

DYSART: No, what? You tell me.

HESTHER [*rising: smiling*]: I won't be put on the stand like this, Martin. You're really disgraceful! ... [*Pause.*] You know what I mean by a normal smile in a child's eyes, and one that isn't – even if I can't exactly define it. Don't you?

DYSART: Yes.

HESTHER: Then we have a duty to that, surely? Both of us.

DYSART: *Touché* ... I'll talk to you.

HESTHER: Dismissed?

DYSART: You said you had to go.

HESTHER: I do ... [*She kisses his cheek.*] Thank you for what you're doing ... You're going through a rotten patch at the moment. I'm sorry ... I suppose one of the few things one can do is simply hold on to priorities.

DYSART: Like what?

HESTHER: Oh – children before grown-ups. Things like that.

[*He contemplates her.*]

DYSART: You're really quite splendid.

HESTHER: Famous for it. Good night.

[*She leaves him.*]

DYSART [*to himself – or to the audience*]: Normal! ... Normal!

19

[ALAN *rises and enters the square. He is subdued.*]

DYSART: Good afternoon.

ALAN: Afternoon.

DYSART: I'm sorry about our row yesterday.

ALAN: It was stupid.

DYSART: It was.

ALAN: What I said, I mean.

DYSART: How are you sleeping?

[ALAN *shrugs.*]

You're not feeling well, are you?

ALAN: All right.

DYSART: Would you like to play a game? It could make you feel better.

ALAN: What kind?

DYSART: It's called *Blink*. You have to fix your eyes on something: say, that little stain over there on the wall – and I tap this pen on the desk. The first time I tap it, you close your eyes. The next time you open them. And so on. Close, open, close, open, till I say stop.

ALAN: How can that make you feel better?

DYSART: It relaxes you. You'll feel as though you're talking to me in your sleep.

ALAN: It's stupid.

DYSART: You don't have to do it, if you don't want to.

ALAN: I didn't say I didn't want to.

DYSART: Well?

ALAN: I don't mind.

DYSART: Good. Sit down and start watching that stain. Put your hands by your sides, and open the fingers wide.

[*He opens the left bench and* ALAN *sits on the end of it.*]

The thing is to feel comfortable, and relax absolutely . . . Are you looking at the stain?

ALAN: Yes.

DYSART: Right. Now try and keep your mind as blank as possible.

ALAN: That's not difficult.

DYSART: Ssh. Stop talking . . . On the first tap, close. On the second, open. Are you ready?

[ALAN *nods.* DYSART *taps his pen on the wooden rail.* ALAN *shuts his eyes.* DYSART *taps again.* ALAN *opens them. The taps are evenly spaced. After four of them the sound cuts out, and is replaced by a louder, metallic sound, on tape.* DYSART *talks through this, to the audience – the light changes to cold – while the boy sits in front of him, staring at the wall, opening and shutting his eyes.*]

The Normal is the good smile in a child's eyes – all right. It is also the dead stare in a million adults. It both sustains and kills – like a God. It is the Ordinary made beautiful; it is also the Average made lethal. The Normal is the indispensable, murderous God of Health, and I am his Priest. My tools are very delicate. My compassion is honest. I have honestly assisted children in this room. I have talked away terrors and relieved many agonies. But also – beyond question – I have cut from them parts of individuality repugnant to this God, in both his aspects. Parts sacred to rarer and more wonderful Gods. And at what length . . . Sacrifices to Zeus took at the most, surely, sixty seconds each. Sacrifices to the Normal can take as long as sixty months.

[*The natural sound of the pencil resumes.*
Light changes back.]

[*To* ALAN.] Now your eyes are feeling heavy. You want to sleep, don't you? You want a long, deep sleep. Have it. Your head is heavy. Very heavy. Your shoulders are heavy. Sleep.

[*The pencil stops.* ALAN's *eyes remain shut and his head has sunk on his chest.*]

Can you hear me?

ALAN: Mmm.

DYSART: You can speak normally. Say Yes, if you can.

ALAN: Yes.

DYSART: Good boy. Now raise your head, and open your eyes.
[*He does so.*]
Now, Alan, you're going to answer questions I'm going to ask you. Do you understand?

ALAN: Yes.

DYSART: And when you wake up, you are going to remember everything you tell me. All right?

ALAN: Yes.

DYSART: Good. Now I want you to think back in time. You are on

that beach you told me about. The tide has gone out, and you're
making sandcastles. Above you, staring down at you, is that great
horse's head, and the cream dropping from it. Can you see that?

ALAN: Yes.

DYSART: You ask him a question. 'Does the chain hurt?'

ALAN: Yes.

DYSART: Do you ask him aloud?

ALAN: No.

DYSART: And what does the horse say back?

ALAN: 'Yes.'

DYSART: Then what do you say?

ALAN: 'I'll take it out for you.'

DYSART: And he says?

ALAN: 'It never comes out. They have me in chains.

DYSART: Like Jesus?

ALAN: Yes!

DYSART: Only his name isn't Jesus, is it?

ALAN: No.

DYSART: What is it?

ALAN: No one knows but him and me.

DYSART: You can tell me, Alan. Name him.

ALAN: Equus.

DYSART: Thank you. Does he live in all horses or just some?

ALAN: All.

DYSART: Good boy. Now: you leave the beach. You're in your bedroom at home. You're twelve years old. You're in front of the
picture. You're looking at Equus from the foot of your bed.
Would you like to kneel down?

ALAN: Yes.

DYSART [encouragingly]: Go on, then.

     [ALAN kneels.]

Now tell me. Why is Equus in chains?

ALAN: For the sins of the world.

DYSART: What does he say to you?

ALAN: 'I see you.' 'I will save you.'

66

DYSART: How?

ALAN: 'Bear you away. Two shall be one.'

DYSART: Horse and rider shall be one beast?

ALAN: One person!

DYSART: Go on.

ALAN: 'And my chinkle-chankle shall be in thy hand.'

DYSART: Chinkle-chankle? That's his mouth chain?

ALAN: Yes.

DYSART: Good. You can get up . . . Come on.
   [ALAN rises.]
   Now: think of the stable. What is the stable? His Temple? His
   Holy of Holies?

ALAN: Yes.

DYSART: Where you wash him? Where you tend him, and brush
   him with many brushes?

ALAN: Yes.

DYSART: And there he spoke to you, didn't he? He looked at you
   with his gentle eyes, and spake unto you?

ALAN: Yes.

DYSART: What did he say? 'Ride me?' 'Mount me, and ride me
   forth at night?'

ALAN: Yes.

DYSART: And you obeyed?

ALAN: Yes.

DYSART: How did you learn? By watching others?

ALAN: Yes.

DYSART: It must have been difficult. You bounced about?

ALAN: Yes.

DYSART: But he showed you, didn't he? Equus showed you the way.

ALAN: No!

DYSART: He didn't?

ALAN: He showed me nothing! He's a mean bugger! Ride – or fall!
   That's Straw Law.

DYSART: Straw Law?

ALAN: He was born in the straw, and this is his law.

DYSART: But you managed? You mastered him?

ALAN: Had to!

DYSART: And then you rode in secret?

ALAN: Yes.

DYSART: How often?

ALAN: Every three weeks. More, people would notice.

DYSART: On a particular horse?

ALAN: No.

DYSART: How did you get into the stable?

ALAN: Stole a key. Had it copied at Bryson's.

DYSART: Clever boy.

> [ALAN *smiles.*]

Then you'd slip out of the house?

ALAN: Midnight! On the stroke!

DYSART: How far's the stable?

ALAN: Two miles.

> [*Pause.*]

DYSART: Let's do it! Let's go riding! ... Now!

> [*He stands up, and pushes in his bench.*]

You are there now, in front of the stable door.

> [ALAN *turns upstage.*]

That key's in your hand. Go and open it.

20

> [ALAN *moves upstage, and mimes opening the door.*
> *Soft light on the circle.*
> *Humming from the* CHORUS: *the Equus noise.*
> *The horse actors enter, raise high their masks, and put them on all together. They stand around the circle –* NUGGET *in the mouth of the tunnel.*]

DYSART: Quietly as possible. Dalton may still be awake. Sssh ...
Quietly ... Good. Now go in.

> [ALAN *steps secretly out of the square through the central opening on to*

the circle, now glowing with a warm light. He looks about him. The
horses stamp uneasily; their masks turn towards him.]

You are on the inside now. All the horses are staring at you. Can
you see them?

ALAN [*excited*]: Yes!

DYSART: Which one are you going to take?

ALAN: Nugget.

[ALAN *reaches up and mimes leading* NUGGET *carefully round the*
circle downstage with a rope, past all the horses on the right.]

DYSART: What colour is Nugget?

ALAN: Chestnut.

[*The horse picks his way with care.* ALAN *halts him at the corner of*
the square.]

DYSART: What do you do, first thing?

ALAN: Put on his sandals.

DYSART: Sandals?

[*He kneels, downstage centre.*]

ALAN: Sandals of majesty! . . . Made of sack.

[*He picks up the invisible sandals, and kisses them devoutly.*]

Tie them round his hooves.

[*He taps* NUGGET's *right leg; the horse raises it and the boy mimes*
tying the sack round it.]

DYSART: All four hooves?

ALAN: Yes.

DYSART: Then?

ALAN: Chinkle-chankle.

[*He mimes picking up the bridle and bit.*]

He doesn't like it so late, but he takes it for my sake. He bends for
me. He stretches forth his neck to it.

[NUGGET *bends his head down.* ALAN *first ritually puts the bit into*
his own mouth, then crosses, and transfers it into NUGGET's. *He*
reaches up and buckles on the bridle. Then he leads him by the in-
visible reins, across the front of the stage and up round the left side of the
circle. NUGGET *follows obediently.*]

ALAN: Buckle and lead out.

DYSART: No saddle?

ALAN: Never.

DYSART: Go on.

ALAN: Walk down the path behind. He's quiet. Always is, this bit. Meek and mild legs. At least till the field. Then there's trouble.

[*The horse jerks back. The mask tosses.*]

DYSART: What kind?

ALAN: Won't go in.

DYSART: Why not?

ALAN: It's his place of Ha Ha.

DYSART: What?

ALAN: Ha Ha.

DYSART: Make him go into it.

ALAN [*whispering fiercely*]: Come on! . . . Come on! . . .

[*He drags the horse into the square as DYSART steps out of it.*]

21

[*NUGGET comes to a halt staring diagonally down what is now the field. The Equus noise dies away. The boy looks about him.*]

DYSART [*from the circle*]: Is it a big field?

ALAN: Huge!

DYSART: What's it like?

ALAN: Full of mist. Nettles on your feet.

[*He mimes taking off his shoes – and the sting.*]
Ah!

DYSART [*going back to his bench*]: You take your shoes off?

ALAN: Everything.

DYSART: All your clothes?

ALAN: Yes.

[*He mimes undressing completely in front of the horse. When he is finished, and obviously quite naked, he throws out his arms and shows himself fully to his God, bowing his head before NUGGET.*]

DYSART: Where do you leave them?

ALAN: Tree hole near the gate. No one could find them.

[*He walks upstage and crouches by the bench, stuffing the invisible clothes beneath it.* DYSART *sits again on the left bench, downstage beyond the circle.*]

DYSART: How does it feel now?

ALAN [*holds himself*]: Burns.

DYSART: Burns?

ALAN: The mist!

DYSART: Go on. Now what?

ALAN: The Manbit.

[*He reaches again under the bench and draws out an invisible stick.*]

DYSART: Manbit?

ALAN: The stick for my mouth.

DYSART: Your mouth?

ALAN: To bite on.

DYSART: Why? What for?

ALAN: So's it won't happen too quick.

DYSART: Is it always the same stick?

ALAN: Course. Sacred stick. Keep it in the hole. The Ark of the Manbit.

DYSART: And now what? . . . What do you do now?

[*Pause. He rises and approaches* NUGGET.]

ALAN: Touch him!

DYSART: Where?

ALAN [*in wonder*]: All over. Everywhere. Belly. Ribs. His ribs are of ivory. Of great value! . . . His flank is cool. His nostrils open for me. His eyes shine. They can see in the dark . . . *Eyes!* –

[*Suddenly he dashes in distress to the farthest corner of the square.*]

DYSART: *Go on!* . . . Then?

[*Pause.*]

ALAN: Give sugar.

DYSART: A lump of sugar?

[ALAN *returns to* NUGGET.]

ALAN: His Last Supper.

DYSART: Last before what?

ALAN: Ha Ha.

[*He kneels before the horse, palms upward and joined together.*]

DYSART: Do you say anything when you give it to him?

ALAN [*offering it*]: Take my sins. Eat them for my sake . . . He always does.

[NUGGET *bows the mask into* ALAN's *palm, then takes a step back to eat.*]

And then he's ready.

DYSART: You can get up on him now?

ALAN: Yes!

DYSART: Do it, then. Mount him.

[ALAN, *lying before* NUGGET, *stretches out on the square. He grasps the top of the thin metal pole embedded in the wood. He whispers his God's name ceremonially.*]

ALAN: Equus! . . . Equus! . . . Equus!

[*He pulls the pole upright. The actor playing* NUGGET *leans forward and grabs it. At the same instant all the other horses lean forward around the circle, each placing a gloved hand on the rail.* ALAN *rises and walks right back to the upstage corner, left.*]

Take me!

[*He runs and jumps high on to* NUGGET's *back.*]

[*Crying out.*] Ah!

DYSART: What is it?

ALAN: Hurts!

DYSART: Hurts?

ALAN: Knives in his skin! Little knives – all inside my legs.

[NUGGET *mimes restiveness.*]

ALAN: Stay, Equus. No one said Go! . . . That's it. He's good. Equus the Godslave, Faithful and True. Into my hands he commends himself – naked in his chinkle-chankle. [*He punches* NUGGET.] Stop it! . . . He wants to go so badly.

DYSART: Go, then. Leave me behind. Ride away now, Alan. Now! . . . Now you are alone with Equus.

[ALAN *stiffens his body.*]

ALAN [*ritually*]: Equus – son of Fleckwus – son of Neckwus – *Walk*.
[*A hum from the* CHORUS.

*Very slowly the horses standing on the circle begin to turn the square
by gently pushing the wooden rail.* ALAN *and his mount start to
revolve. The effect, immediately, is of a statue being slowly turned
round on a plinth. During the ride however the speed increases, and the
light decreases until it is only a fierce spotlight on horse and rider, with
the overspill glinting on the other masks leaning in towards them.*]

Here we go. The King rides out on Equus, mightiest of horses.
Only I can ride him. He lets me turn him this way and that. His
neck comes out of my body. It lifts in the dark. Equus, my Godslave! . . . Now the King commands you. Tonight, we ride against
them all.

DYSART: Who's all?

ALAN: My foes and His.

DYSART: Who are your foes?

ALAN: The Hosts of Hoover. The Hosts of Philco. The Hosts of
Pifco. The House of Remington and all its tribe!

DYSART: Who are His foes?

ALAN: The Hosts of Jodhpur. The Hosts of Bowler and Gymkhana.
All those who show him off for their vanity. Tie rosettes on his
head for their vanity! Come on, Equus. Let's get them! . . . *Trot!*

[*The speed of the turning square increases.*]

Stead-y! Stead-y! Stead-y! Stead-y! Cowboys are watching! Take
off their stetsons. They know who we are. They're admiring us!
Bowing low unto us! Come on now – show them! *Canter!* . . .
CANTER!

[*He whips* NUGGET.]

And Equus the Mighty rose against All!
His enemies scatter, his enemies fall!
TURN!
Trample them, trample them,
Trample them, trample them,
TURN!

TURN!!
TURN!!!

[*The Equus noise increases in volume.*]

[*Shouting.*] WEE!... WAA!... WONDERFUL!...

I'm stiff! Stiff in the wind!

My mane, stiff in the wind!

My flanks! *My* hooves!

Mane on my legs, on my flanks, like whips!

Raw!

Raw!

I'm raw! Raw!

Feel me on you! *On* you! *On* you! *On* you!

I want to be *in* you!

I want to BE you forever and ever! –

Equus, I love you!

Now! –

Bear me away!

Make us One Person!

[*He rides* EQUUS *frantically.*]

One Person! One Person! One Person! One Person!

[*He rises up on the horse's back, and calls like a trumpet.*]

Ha-HA!... Ha-HA!... Ha-HA!

[*The trumpet turns to great cries.*]

HA-HA! HA-HA! HA-HA! HA-HA! HA!... HA!...
HAAAAA!

[*He twists like a flame.*

Silence.

The turning square comes to a stop in the same position it occupied at the opening of the Act.

Slowly the boy drops off the horse's back on to the ground.

He lowers his head and kisses NUGGET's *hoof.*

Finally he flings back his head and cries up to him.]

AMEN!

[NUGGET *snorts, once.*]

BLACKOUT

74

ACT TWO

22

Darkness.
Lights come slowly up on ALAN *kneeling in the night at the hooves of*
NUGGET. *Slowly he gets up, climbing lovingly up the body of the horse*
until he can stand and kiss it.
DYSART *sits on the downstage bench where he began Act One.*

DYSART: With one particular horse, called Nugget, he embraces. He
  showed me how he stands with it afterwards in the night, one hand
  on its chest, one on its neck, like a frozen tango dancer, inhaling its
  cold sweet breath. 'Have you noticed', he said, 'about horses: how
  they'll stand one hoof on its end, like those girls in the ballet?'
    [ALAN *leads* NUGGET *out of the square.* DYSART *rises. The horse*
    walks away up the tunnel and disappears. The boy comes downstage
    and sits on the bench DYSART *has vacated.* DYSART *crosses down-*
    stage and moves slowly up round the circle, until he reaches the central
    entrance to the square.]
  Now he's gone off to rest, leaving me alone with Equus. I can hear
  the creature's voice. It's calling me out of the black cave of the
  Psyche. I shove in my dim little torch, and there he stands – waiting
  for me. He raises his matted head. He opens his great square teeth,
  and says – [*Mocking.*] '*Why?* . . . Why Me? . . . Why – ultimately –
  Me? . . . Do you really imagine you can account for Me? Totally,
  infallibly, inevitably account for Me? . . . Poor Doctor Dysart!'
    [*He enters the square.*]
  Of course I've stared at such images before. Or been stared at by
  them, whichever way you look at it. And weirdly often now with
  me the feeling is that *they* are staring at *us* – that in some quite

75

palpable way they precede us. Meaningless, but unsettling . . . In either case, this one is the most alarming yet. It asks questions I've avoided all my professional life. [*Pause.*] A child is born into a world of phenomena all equal in their power to enslave. It sniffs – it sucks – it strokes its eyes over the whole uncomfortable range. Suddenly one strikes. Why? Moments snap together like magnets, forging a chain of shackles. Why? I can trace them. I can even, with time, pull them apart again. But why at the start they were ever magnetized at all – just those particular moments of experience and no others – I don't know. *And nor does anyone else.* Yet *if* I don't know – if I can never know that – then what am I doing here? I don't mean clinically doing or socially doing – I mean *fundamentally*! These questions, these Whys, are fundamental – yet they have no place in a consulting room. So then, do I? . . . This is the feeling more and more with me – No Place. Displacement . . . 'Account for me,' says staring Equus. 'First account for Me! . . .' I fancy this is more than menopause.

[NURSE *rushes in.*]

NURSE: Doctor! . . . Doctor! There's a terrible scene with the Strang boy. His mother came to visit him, and I gave her the tray to take in. He threw it at her. She's saying the most dreadful things.

[ALAN *springs up, down left.* DORA *springs up, down right. They face each other across the bottom end of the stage. It is observable that at the start of this Act* FRANK *is not sitting beside his wife on their bench. It is hopefully not observable that he is placed among the audience upstage, in the gloom, by the central tunnel.*]

DORA: Don't you dare! *Don't you dare!*

DYSART: Is she still there?

NURSE: Yes!

[*He quickly leaves the square, followed by the* NURSE. DORA *moves towards her son.*]

DORA: Don't you look at me like that! I'm not a doctor, you know, who'll take anything. Don't you dare give me that stare, young man!

[*She slaps his face.* DYSART *joins them.*]

DYSART: Mrs Strang!

DORA: I know your stares. They don't work on me!

DYSART [to her]: Leave this room.

DORA: What did you say?

DYSART: I tell you to leave here at once.

[DORA hesitates. Then:]

DORA: Good-bye, Alan.

[She walks past her son, and round into the square. DYSART follows her. Both are very upset. ALAN returns to his bench and NURSE to her place.]

23

[Lights up on the square.]

DYSART: I must ask you never to come here again.

DORA: Do you think I want to? Do you think I want to?

DYSART: Mrs Strang, what on earth has got into you? Can't you see the boy is highly distressed?

DORA [ironic]: Really?

DYSART: Of course! He's at a most delicate stage of treatment. He's totally exposed. Ashamed. Everything you can imagine!

DORA [exploding]: And me? What about me? . . . What do you think I am? . . . I'm a parent, of course – so it doesn't count. That's a dirty word in here, isn't it, 'parent'?

DYSART: You know that's not true.

DORA: Oh, I know. I know, all right! I've heard it all my life. It's our fault. Whatever happens, we did it. Alan's just a little victim. He's really done nothing at all! [Savagely.] What do you have to do in this world to get any sympathy – blind animals?

DYSART: Sit down, Mrs Strang.

DORA [ignoring him: more and more urgently]: Look, Doctor: you don't have to live with this. Alan is one patient to you: one out of many. He's my son. I lie awake every night thinking about it. Frank lies there beside me. I can hear him. Neither of us sleeps all

77

night. You come to us and say, who forbids television? who does what behind whose back? – as if we're criminals. Let me tell you something. We're not criminals. We've done nothing wrong. We loved Alan. We gave him the best love we could. All right, we quarrel sometimes – all parents quarrel – we always make it up. My husband is a good man. He's an upright man, religion or no religion. He cares for his home, for the world, and for his boy. Alan had love and care and treats, and as much fun as any boy in the world. I know about loveless homes: I was a teacher. Our home wasn't loveless. I know about privacy too – not invading a child's privacy. All right, Frank may be at fault there – he digs into him too much – but nothing in excess. He's not a bully . . . [*Gravely.*] No, doctor. Whatever's happened has happened *because of Alan.* Alan is himself. Every soul is itself. If you added up everything we ever did to him, from his first day on earth to this, you wouldn't find why he did this terrible thing – because that's *him*; not just all of our things added up. Do you understand what I'm saying? I want you to understand, because I lie awake and awake thinking it out, and I want you to know that I deny it absolutely what he's doing now, staring at me, attacking me for what *he's* done, for what *he* is! [*Pause: calmer.*] You've got your words, and I've got mine. You call it a complex, I suppose. But if you knew God, Doctor, you would know about the Devil. You'd know the Devil isn't made by what mummy says and daddy says. The Devil's *there.* It's an old-fashioned word, but a true thing . . . I'll go. What I did in there was inexcusable. I only know he was my little Alan, and then the Devil came.

[*She leaves the square, and resumes her place.* DYSART *watches her go, then leaves himself by the opposite entrance, and approaches* ALAN.]

[*Seated on his bench, the boy glares at him.*]

DYSART: I thought you liked your mother.

[*Silence.*]

She doesn't know anything, you know. I haven't told her what you told me. You do know that, don't you?

ALAN: It was lies anyway.

DYSART: What?

ALAN: You and your pencil. Just a con trick, that's all.

DYSART: What do you mean?

ALAN: Made me say a lot of lies.

DYSART: Did it? . . . Like what?

ALAN: All of it. Everything I said. Lot of lies.

[*Pause.*]

DYSART: I see.

ALAN: You ought to be locked up. Your bloody tricks.

DYSART: I thought you liked tricks.

ALAN: It'll be the drug next. I know.

[DYSART *turns, sharply.*]

DYSART: What drug?

ALAN: I've heard. I'm not ignorant. I know what you get up to in here. Shove needles in people, pump them full of truth drug, so they can't help saying things. That's next, isn't it?

[*Pause.*]

DYSART: Alan, do you know why you're here?

ALAN: So you can give me truth drugs.

[*He glares at him.*

DYSART *leaves abruptly, and returns to the square.*]

[HESTHER *comes in simultaneously from the other side.*]

DYSART [*agitated*]: He actually thinks they exist! And of course he wants one.

HESTHER: It doesn't sound like that to me.

DYSART: Of course he does. Why mention them otherwise? He wants a way to speak. To finally tell me what happened in that stable. Tape's too isolated, and hypnosis is a trick. At least that's the pretence.

HESTHER: Does he still say that today?

DYSART: I haven't seen him. I cancelled his appointment this morning, and let him stew in his own anxiety. Now I am almost tempted to play a real trick on him.

HESTHER [*sitting*]: Like what?

DYSART: The old placebo.

HESTHER: You mean a harmless pill?

DYSART: Full of *alleged* Truth Drug. Probably an aspirin.

HESTHER: But he'd deny it afterwards. Same thing all over.

DYSART: No. Because he's ready to abreact.

HESTHER: Abreact?

DYSART: Live it all again. He won't be able to deny it after that, because he'll have shown me. Not just told me – but acted it out in front of me.

HESTHER: Can you get him to do that?

DYSART: I think so. He's nearly done it already. Under all that glowering, he trusts me. Do you realize that?

HESTHER [*warmly*]: I'm sure he does.

DYSART: Poor bloody fool.

HESTHER: Don't start that again.

[*Pause.*]

DYSART [*quietly*]: Can you think of anything worse one can do to anybody than take away their worship?

HESTHER: Worship?

DYSART: Yes, that word again!

HESTHER: Aren't you being a little extreme?

DYSART: Extremity's the point.

HESTHER: Worship isn't destructive, Martin. I know that.

DYSART: I don't. I only know it's the core of his life. What else has he got? Think about him. He can hardly read. He knows no physics or engineering to make the world real for him. No paintings to show him how others have enjoyed it. No music except television jingles. No history except tales from a desperate mother. No friends. Not one kid to give him a joke, or make him know himself more moderately. He's a modern citizen for whom society doesn't exist. He lives *one hour* every three weeks – howling in a mist. And after the service kneels to a slave who stands over him obviously and unthrowably his master. With my body I thee worship! . . . Many men have less vital with their wives.

 [*Pause.*]

HESTHER: All the same, they don't usually blind their wives, do they?

DYSART: Oh, come on!

HESTHER: Well, do they?

DYSART [*sarcastically*]: You mean he's dangerous? A violent, dangerous madman who's going to run round the country doing it again and again?

HESTHER: I mean he's in pain, Martin. He's been in pain for most of his life. That much, at least, you *know*.

DYSART: Possibly.

HEATHER: *Possibly?!* . . . That cut-off little figure you just described must have been in pain for years.

DYSART [*doggedly*]: Possibly.

HESTHER: And you can take it away.

DYSART: Still – possibly.

HESTHER: Then that's enough. That simply has to be enough for you, surely?

DYSART: No!

HESTHER: Why not?

DYSART: Because it's his.

HESTHER: I don't understand.

DYSART: His pain. His own. He made it.

[*Pause.*]

[*Earnestly.*] Look ... to go through life and call it yours – *your life* – you first have to get your own pain. Pain that's unique to you. You can't just dip into the common bin and say 'That's enough!' ... He's done that. All right, he's sick. He's full of misery and fear. He was dangerous, and could be again, though I doubt it. But that boy has known a passion more ferocious than I have felt in any second of my life. And let me tell you something: I envy it.

HESTHER: You can't.

DYSART [*vehemently*]: Don't you see? That's the Accusation! That's what his stare has been saying to me all this time. '*At least I galloped! When did you?*' ... [*Simply.*] I'm jealous, Hesther. Jealous of Alan Strang.

ESTHER: That's absurd.

YSART: Is it? ... I go on about my wife. That smug woman by the fire. Have you thought of the fellow on the other side of it? The finicky, critical husband looking through his art books on mythical Greece. What worship has *he* ever known? Real worship! Without worship you shrink, it's as brutal as that ... I shrank my *own* life. No one can do it for you. I settled for being pallid and provincial, out of my own eternal timidity. The old story of bluster, and do bugger-all ... I imply that we can't have children; but actually, it's only me. I had myself tested behind her back. The lowest sperm count you could find. And I never told her. That's all I need – her sympathy mixed with resentment ... I tell everyone Margaret's the puritan, I'm the pagan. Some pagan! Such wild returns I make to the womb of civilization. Three weeks a year in the Peleponnese, every bed booked in advance, every meal paid for by vouchers, cautious jaunts in hired Fiats, suitcase crammed with Kao-Pectate! Such a fantastic surrender to the primitive. And I use that word endlessly: 'primitive'. 'Oh, the primitive world,' I say. 'What instinctual truths were lost with it!' And while I sit there, baiting a poor unimaginative woman with the word, that freaky boy tries to conjure the reality! I sit looking at pages of centaurs trampling the soil of Argos – and outside my window he is trying to *become one*, in a Hampshire field! . . . I watch that woman knitting, night after night – a woman I haven't *kissed* in six years – and he stands in the dark for an hour, sucking the sweat off his God's hairy cheek! [*Pause.*] Then in the morning, I put away my books on the cultural shelf, close up the kodachrome snaps of Mount Olympus, touch my reproduction statue of Dionysus for luck – and go off to hospital to treat him for insanity. Do you see?

HESTHER: The boy's in pain, Martin. That's all I see. In the end . . . I'm sorry.

> [*He looks at her.* ALAN *gets up from his bench and stealthily places an envelope in the left-hand entrance of the square, then goes back and sits with his back to the audience, as if watching television.*
>
> HESTHER *rises.*]

HESTHER: That stare of his. Have you thought it might not be accusing you at all?

DYSART: What then?

HESTHER: Claiming you.

DYSART: For what?

HESTHER [*mischievously*]: A new God.

> [*Pause.*]

DYSART: Too conventional, for him. Finding a religion in Psychiatry is really for very ordinary patients.

> [*She laughs.*]

HESTHER: Maybe he just wants a new Dad. Or is that too conventional too? . . . Since you're questioning your profession anyway, perhaps you ought to try it and see.

DYSART [*amused*]: I'll talk to you.

HESTHER: Goodbye.

> [*She smiles, and leaves him.*]

[DYSART *becomes aware of the letter lying on the floor. He picks it up, opens and reads it.*]

ALAN [*speaking stiffly, as* DYSART *reads*]: 'It is all true, what I said after you tapped the pencil. I'm sorry if I said different. Post Scriptum: I know why I'm in here.'

[*Pause.*]

DYSART [*calling, joyfully*]: Nurse!

[NURSE *comes in.*]

NURSE: Yes, Doctor?

DYSART [*trying to conceal his pleasure*]: Good evening!

NURSE: You're in late tonight.

DYSART: Yes! . . . Tell me, is the Strang boy in bed yet?

NURSE: Oh, no, Doctor. He's bound to be upstairs looking at television. He always watches to the last possible moment. He doesn't like going to his room at all.

DYSART: You mean he's still having nightmares?

NURSE: He had a bad one last night.

DYSART: Would you ask him to come down here, please?

NURSE [*faint surprise*]: Now?

DYSART: I'd like a word with him.

NURSE [*puzzled*]: Very good, Doctor.

DYSART: If he's not back in his room by lights out, tell Night Nurse not to worry. I'll see he gets back to bed all right. And would you phone my home and tell my wife I may be in late?

NURSE: Yes, Doctor.

DYSART: Ask him to come straight away, please.

[NURSE *goes to the bench, taps* ALAN *on the shoulder, whispers her message in his ear, and returns to her place.* ALAN *stands up and pauses for a second – then steps into the square.*]

[*He stands in the doorway, depressed.*]

DYSART: Hallo.

ALAN: Hallo.

DYSART: I got your letter. Thank you. [*Pause.*] Also the Post Scriptum.

ALAN [*defensively*]: That's the right word. My mum told me. It's Latin for 'After-writing'.

DYSART: How are you feeling?

ALAN: All right.

DYSART: I'm sorry I didn't see you today.

ALAN: You were fed up with me.

DYSART: Yes. [*Pause.*] Can I make it up to you now?

ALAN: What d'you mean?

DYSART: I thought we'd have a session

ALAN [*startled*]: Now?

DYSART: Yes! At dead of night! ... Better than going to sleep, isn't it?

    [*The boy flinches.*]

Alan – look. Everything I say has a trick or a catch. Everything I do is a trick or a catch. That's all I know to do. But they work – and you know that. Trust me.

    [*Pause.*]

ALAN: You got another trick, then?

DYSART: Yes.

ALAN: A truth drug?

DYSART: If you like.

ALAN: What's it do?

DYSART: Make it easier for you to talk.

ALAN: Like you can't help yourself?

DYSART: That's right. Like you have to speak the truth at all costs. And all of it.

    [*Pause.*]

ALAN [*slyly*]: Comes in a needle, doesn't it?

DYSART: No.

ALAN: Where is it?

DYSART [*indicating his pocket*]: In here.

ALAN: Let's see.

[*DYSART solemnly takes a bottle of pills out of his pocket.*]

DYSART: There.

ALAN [*suspicious*]: That really it?

DYSART: It is . . . Do you want to try it?

ALAN: No.

DYSART: I think you do.

ALAN: I don't. Not at all.

DYSART: Afterwards you'd sleep. You'd have no bad dreams all night. Probably many nights, from then on . . .

[*Pause.*]

ALAN: How long's it take to work?

DYSART: It's instant. Like coffee.

ALAN [*half believing*]: It isn't!

DYSART: I promise you . . . Well?

ALAN: Can I have a fag?

DYSART: Pill first. Do you want some water?

ALAN: No.

[*DYSART shakes one out on to his palm. ALAN hesitates for a second – then takes it and swallows it.*]

DYSART: Then you can chase it down with this. Sit down.

[*He offers him a cigarette, and lights it for him.*]

ALAN [*nervous*]: What happens now?

DYSART: We wait for it to work.

ALAN: What'll I feel first?

DYSART: Nothing much. After a minute, about a hundred green snakes should come out of that cupboard singing the Hallelujah Chorus.

ALAN [*annoyed*]: I'm serious!

DYSART [*earnestly*]: You'll feel nothing. Nothing's going to happen now but what you want to happen. You're not going to say anything to me but what you want to say. Just relax. Lie back and finish your fag.

[ALAN *stares at him. Then accepts the situation, and lies back.*]

DYSART: Good boy.

ALAN: I bet this room's heard some funny things.

DYSART: It certainly has.

ALAN: I like it.

DYSART: This room?

ALAN: Don't you?

DYSART: Well, there's not much to like, is there?

ALAN: How long am I going to be in here?

DYSART: It's hard to say. I quite see you want to leave.

ALAN: No.

DYSART: You don't?

ALAN: Where would I go?

DYSART: Home . . .

[*The boy looks at him.* DYSART *crosses and sits on the rail upstage, his feet on the bench. A pause.*]

Actually, I'd like to leave this room and never see it again in my life.

ALAN [*surprise*]: Why?

DYSART: I've been in it too long.

ALAN: Where would you go?

DYSART: Somewhere.

ALAN: Secret?

DYSART: Yes. There's a sea – a great sea – I love . . . It's where the Gods used to go to bathe.

ALAN: What Gods?

DYSART: The old ones. Before they died.

ALAN: Gods don't die.

DYSART: Yes, they do.

[*Pause.*]

There's a village I spent one night in, where I'd like to live. It's all white.

ALAN: How would you Nosey Parker, though? You wouldn't have a room for it any more.

87

DYSART: I wouldn't mind. I don't actually enjoy being a Nosey Parker, you know.

ALAN: Then why do it?

DYSART: Because you're unhappy.

ALAN: So are you.

[DYSART *looks at him sharply.* ALAN *sits up in alarm.*]

Oooh, I didn't mean that!

DYSART: Didn't you?

ALAN: Here – is that how it works? Things just slip out, not feeling anything?

DYSART: That's right.

ALAN: But it's so quick!

DYSART: I told you; it's instant.

ALAN [*delighted*]: It's wicked, isn't it? I mean, you can say anything under it.

DYSART: Yes.

ALAN: Ask me a question.

DYSART: Tell me about Jill.

[*Pause. The boy turns away.*]

ALAN: There's nothing to tell.

DYSART: Nothing?

ALAN: No.

DYSART: Well, for example – is she pretty? You've never described her.

ALAN: She's all right.

DYSART: What colour hair?

ALAN: Dunno.

DYSART: Is it long or short?

ALAN: Dunno.

DYSART [*lightly*]: You must know that.

ALAN: I don't remember. *I don't!*

[DYSART *rises and comes down to him. He takes the cigarette out of his hand.*]

DYSART [*firmly*]: Lie back . . . Now listen. You have to do this. And now. You are going to tell me everything that happened with this

88

girl. And not just *tell* me – *show* me. Act it out, if you like – even more than you did when I tapped the pencil. I want you to feel free to do absolutely anything in this room. The pill will help you. I will help you . . . Now, where does she live?

[*A long pause.*]

ALAN [*tight*]: Near the stables. About a mile.

[DYSART *steps down out of the square as* JILL *enters it. He sits again on the downstage bench.*]

28

[*The light grows warmer.*]

JILL: It's called The China Pantry.

[*She comes down and sits casually on the rail. Her manner is open and lightly provocative. During these scenes* ALAN *acts directly with her, and never looks over at* DYSART *when he replies to him.*]

When Daddy disappeared, she was left without a bean. She had to earn her own living. I must say she did jolly well, considering she was never trained in business.

DYSART: What do you mean, 'disappeared'?

ALAN [*to* DYSART]: He ran off. No one ever saw him again.

JILL: Just left a note on her dressing table saying 'Sorry. I've had it.' Just like that. She never got over it. It turned her right off men. All my dates have to be sort of secret. I mean, she knows about them, but I can't ever bring anyone back home. She's so rude to them.

ALAN [*to* DYSART]: She was always looking.

DYSART: At you?

ALAN [*to* DYSART]: Saying stupid things.

[*She jumps off the bench.*]

JILL: You've got super eyes.

ALAN [*to* DYSART]: Anyway, *she* was the one who had them.

[*She sits next to him. Embarrassed, the boy tries to move away as far as he can.*]

JILL: There was an article in the paper last week saying what points about boys fascinate girls. They said Number One is bottoms. I think it's eyes every time ... They fascinate you too, don't they?

ALAN: Me?

JILL [*sly*]: Or is it only horses' eyes?

ALAN [*startled*]: What d'you mean?

JILL: I saw you staring into Nugget's eyes yesterday for ages. I spied on you through the door!

ALAN [*hotly*]: There must have been something in it!

JILL: You're a real Man of Mystery, aren't you?

ALAN [*to* DYSART]: Sometimes, it was like she knew.

DYSART: Did you ever hint?

ALAN [*to* DYSART]: Course not!

JILL: I love horses' eyes. The way you can see yourself in them. D'you find them sexy?

ALAN [*outraged*]: What?!

JILL: Horses.

ALAN: Don't be daft!

[*He springs up, and away from her.*]

JILL: Girls do. I mean, they go through a period when they pat them and kiss them a lot. I know *I* did. I suppose it's just a substitute, really.

ALAN [*to* DYSART]: That kind of thing, all the time. Until one night ...

DYSART: Yes? What?

ALAN [*to* DYSART: *defensively*]: She did it! Not me. It was her idea, the whole thing! ... She got me into it!

DYSART: What are you saying? 'One night': go on from there.

[*A pause.*]

ALAN [*to* DYSART]: Saturday night. We were just closing up.

JILL: How would you like to take me out?

ALAN: What?

JILL [*coolly*]: How would you like to take me out tonight?

ALAN: I've got to go home.

JILL: What for?

[*He tries to escape upstage.*]

ALAN: They expect me.

JILL: Ring up and say you're going out.

ALAN: I can't.

JILL: Why?

ALAN: They expect me.

JILL: Look. Either we go out together and have some fun, or you go back to your boring home, *as usual*, and I go back to mine. That's the situation, isn't it?

ALAN: Well . . . where would we go?

JILL: The pictures! There's a skinflick over in Winchester! I've never seen one, have you?

ALAN: No.

JILL: Wouldn't you like to? *I* would. All those heavy Swedes, panting at each other! . . . What d'you say?

ALAN [*grinning*]: Yeh! . . .

JILL: Good! . . .

[*He turns away.*]

DYSART: Go on, please.

[*He steps off the square.*]

ALAN [*to* DYSART]: I'm tired now!

DYSART: Come on now. You can't stop there.

[*He storms round the circle to* DYSART, *and faces him directly.*]

ALAN: I'm *tired*! I want to go to bed!

DYSART [*sharply*]: Well, you can't. I want to hear about the film.

ALAN [*hostile*]: Hear what? . . . *What?* . . . It was bloody awful!

[*The actors playing horses come swiftly on to the square, dressed in sports coats or raincoats. They move the benches to be parallel with the audience, and sit on them – staring out front.*]

DYSART: Why?

ALAN: Nosey Parker!

DYSART: *Why?*

ALAN: *Because!* . . . Well – we went into the Cinema!

[*A burst of Rock music, instantly fading down. Lights darken.*
ALAN *re-enters the square.* JILL *rises and together they grope their way to the downstage bench, as if in a dark auditorium.*]

ALAN [*to* DYSART]: The whole place was full of men. Jill was the only girl.

[*They push by a patron seated at the end, and sit side by side, staring up at the invisible screen, located above the heads of the main audience. A spotlight hits the boy's face.*]

We sat down and the film came on. It was daft. Nothing happened for ages. There was this girl Brita, who was sixteen. She went to stay in this house, where there was an older boy. He kept giving her looks, but she ignored him completely. In the end she took a shower. She went into the bathroom and took off all her clothes. The lot. Very slowly ... What she didn't know was the boy was looking through the door all the time ... [*He starts to become excited.*] It was fantastic! The water fell on her breasts, bouncing down her ...

[FRANK *steps into the square furtively from the back, hat in hand, and stands looking about for a place.*]

DYSART: Was that the first time you'd seen a girl naked?

ALAN [*to* DYSART]: Yes! You couldn't see everything, though ...
[*Looking about him.*] All round me they were all looking. All the men – staring up like they were in church. Like they were a sort of congregation. And then – [*He sees his father.*] *Ah!*

[*At the same instant* FRANK *sees him.*]

FRANK: Alan!

ALAN: God!

JILL: What is it?

ALAN: *Dad!*

JILL: *Where?*

ALAN: At the back! *He saw me!*

JILL: You sure?

ALAN: Yes!

FRANK [*calling*]: Alan!

ALAN: Oh God!

> [*He tries to hide his face in the girl's shoulder. His father comes down the aisle towards him.*]

FRANK: Alan! You can hear me! Don't pretend!

PATRONS: *Ssssh!*

FRANK [*approaching the row of seats*]: Do I have to come and fetch you out? ... Do I? ...

> [*Cries of 'Sssh!' and 'Shut up!'*]

> Do I, Alan?

ALAN [*through gritted teeth*]: Oh fuck!

> [*He gets up as the noise increases.* JILL *gets up too and follows him.*]

DYSART: You went?

ALAN [*to* DYSART]: What else could I do? He kept shouting. Everyone was saying Shut up!

> [*They go out, right, through the group of* PATRONS – *who rise protesting as they pass, quickly replace the benches and leave the square.* DYSART *enters it.*]

30

> [*Light brightens from the cinema, but remains cold: streets at night. The three walk round the circle downstage in a line:* FRANK *leading, wearing his hat. He halts in the middle of the left rail, and stands staring straight ahead of him, rigid with embarrassment.*
> ALAN *is very agitated.*]

ALAN [*to* DYSART]: We went into the street, all three of us. It was weird. We just stood there by the bus stop – like we were three people in a queue, and we didn't know each other. Dad was all white and sweaty. He didn't look at us at all. It must have gone on for about five minutes. I tried to speak. I said – [*To his father.*] I – I – I've never been there before. Honest ... Never ... [*To* DYSART.] He didn't seem to hear. Jill tried.

JILL: It's true, Mr Strang. It wasn't Alan's idea to go there. It was mine.

ALAN [*to* DYSART]: He just went on staring, straight ahead. It was awful.

JILL: I'm not shocked by films like that. I think they're just silly.

ALAN [*to* DYSART]: The bus wouldn't come. We just stood and stood . . . Then suddenly he spoke.

[FRANK *takes off his hat.*]

FRANK [*stiffly*]: I'd like you to know something. Both of you. I came here tonight to see the Manager. He asked me to call on him for business purposes. I happen to be a printer, Miss. A picture house needs posters. That's entirely why I'm here. To discuss posters. While I was waiting I happened to glance in, that's all. I can only say I'm going to complain to the council. I had no idea they showed films like this. I'm certainly going to refuse my services.

JILL [*kindly*]: Yes, of course.

FRANK: So long as that's understood.

ALAN [*to* DYSART]: Then the bus came along.

FRANK: Come along now, Alan.

[*He moves away downstage.*]

ALAN: No.

FRANK [*turning*]: No fuss, please. Say good night to the young lady.

ALAN [*timid but firm*]: No. I'm stopping here . . . I've got to see her home . . . It's proper.

[*Pause.*]

FRANK [*as dignified as possible*]: Very well. I'll see you when you choose to return. Very well then . . . Yes . . .

[*He walks back to his original seat, next to his wife. He stares across the square at his son – who stares back at him. Then, slowly, he sits.*]

ALAN [*to* DYSART]: And he got in, and we didn't. He sat down and looked at me through the glass. And I saw . . .

DYSART [*soft*]: What?

ALAN [*to* DYSART]: His face. It was scared.

DYSART: Of you?

ALAN [*to* DYSART]: It was terrible. We had to walk home. Four miles. I got the shakes.

DYSART: You were scared too?

ALAN [*to* DYSART]: It was like a hole had been drilled in my tummy. A hole – right here. And the air was getting in!

[*He starts to walk upstage, round the circle.*]

31

[*The girl stays still.*]

JILL [*aware of other people looking*]: Alan . . .

ALAN [*to* DYSART]: People kept turning round in the street to look.

JILL: Alan!

ALAN [*to* DYSART]: I kept seeing him, just as he drove off. Scared of me . . . And me scared of *him* . . . I kept thinking – all those airs he put on! . . . 'Receive my meaning. Improve your mind!' . . . All those nights he said he'd be in late. 'Keep my supper hot, Dora!' 'Your poor father: he works so hard!' . . . Bugger! Old bugger! . . . Filthy old bugger!

[*He stops, clenching his fists.*]

JILL: Hey! Wait for me!

[*She runs after him. He waits.*]

What are you thinking about?

ALAN: Nothing.

JILL: Mind my own beeswax?

[*She laughs.*]

ALAN [*to* DYSART] And suddenly she began to laugh.

JILL: I'm sorry. But it's pretty funny, when you think of it.

ALAN [*bewildered*]: What?

JILL: Catching him like that! I mean, it's terrible – but it's very funny.

ALAN: Yeh!

[*He turns from her.*]

JILL: No, wait! . . . I'm sorry. I know you're upset. But it's not the end of the world, is it? I mean, what was he doing? Only what we were. Watching a silly film. It's a case of like father like son, I'd say! . . . I mean, when that girl was taking a shower, you were pretty interested, weren't you?

[*He turns round and looks at her.*]

We keep saying old people are square. Then when they suddenly aren't – we don't like it!

DYSART: What did you think about that?

ALAN [*to* DYSART]: I don't know. I kept looking at all the people in the street. They were mostly men coming out of pubs. I suddenly thought – *they all do it! All of them!* . . . They're not just Dads – they're people with pricks! . . . And Dad – he's not just Dad either. He's a man with a prick too. You know, I'd never thought about it.

[*Pause.*]

We went into the country.

[*He walks again.* JILL *follows. They turn the corner and come downstage, right.*]

We kept walking. I just thought about Dad, and how he was nothing special – just a poor old sod on his own.

[*He stops.*]

[*To* JILL: *realizing it.*] Poor old sod!

JILL: That's right!

ALAN [*grappling with it*]: I mean, what else has he got? . . . He's got mum, of course, but well – she – she – she –

JILL: She doesn't give him anything?

ALAN: That's right. I bet you . . . She doesn't give him anything. That's right . . . That's really right! . . . She likes Ladies and Gentlemen. Do you understand what I mean?

JILL [*mischievously*]: Ladies and gentlemen aren't naked?

ALAN: That's right! Never! . . . *Never!* That would be disgusting! She'd have to put bowler hats on them! . . . Jodhpurs!

[*She laughs.*]

DYSART: Was that the first time you ever thought anything like that about your mother? . . . I mean, that she was unfair to your dad?

ALAN [*to* DYSART]: Absolutely!

DYSART: How did you feel?

ALAN [*to* DYSART]: Sorry. I mean for him. Poor old sod, that's what I felt – he's just like me! He hates ladies and gents just like me! Posh things – and la-di-da. He goes off by himself at night, and does his own secret thing which no one'll know about, just like me! There's no difference – he's just the same as me – just the same! – [*He stops in distress, then bolts back a little upstage.*] Christ!

DYSART [*sternly*]: Go on.

ALAN [*to* DYSART]: I can't.

DYSART: Of course you can. You're doing wonderfully.

ALAN [*to* DYSART]: No, please. *Don't make me!*

DYSART [*firm*]: Don't think: just answer. You were happy at that second, weren't you? When you realized about your dad. How lots of people have secrets, not just you?

ALAN [*to* DYSART]: Yes.

DYSART: You felt sort of free, didn't you? I mean, free to do anything?

ALAN [*to* DYSART, *looking at* JILL]: Yes!

DYSART: What was she doing?

ALAN [*to* DYSART]: Holding my hand.

DYSART: And that was good?

ALAN [*to* DYSART]: Oh, yes!

DYSART: Remember what you thought. *As if it's happening to you now. This very moment* ... What's in your head?

ALAN [*to* DYSART]: Her eyes. *She's* the one with eyes! ... I keep looking at them, because I really want –

DYSART: To look at her breasts?

ALAN [*to* DYSART]: Yes.

DYSART: Like in the film.

ALAN [*to* DYSART]: Yes ... Then she starts to scratch my hand.

JILL: You're really very nice, you know that?

ALAN [*to* DYSART]: Moving her nails on the back. Her face so warm. Her eyes.

DYSART: You want her very much?

ALAN [*to* DYSART]: Yes ...

JILL: I love your eyes.

   [*She kisses him.*]

  [*Whispering.*] Let's go!

ALAN: Where?

JILL: I know a place. It's right near here.

ALAN: Where?

JILL: Surprise! . . . Come on!

   [*She darts away round the circle, across the stage and up the left side.*]
Come *on*!

ALAN [*to* DYSART]: She runs ahead. I follow. And then – and then –!

   [*He halts.*]

DYSART: What?

ALAN [*to* DYSART]: I see what she means.

DYSART: What? . . . Where are you? . . . Where has she taken
you?

ALAN [*to* JILL]: *The Stables?*

JILL: Of course!

32

   [CHORUS *makes a warning hum.*

   *The horses actors enter, and ceremonially put on their masks – first
raising them high above their heads.* NUGGET *stands in the central
tunnel.*]

ALAN [*recoiling*]: No!

JILL: Where else? They're perfect!

ALAN: No!

   [*He turns his head from her.*]

JILL: Or do you want to go home now and face your dad?

ALAN: No!

JILL: Then come on!

   [*He edges nervously past the horse standing at the left, which turns its
neck and even moves a challenging step after him.*]

ALAN: Why not your place?

JILL: I can't. Mother doesn't like me bringing back boys. I told you ... Anyway, the Barn's better.

ALAN: No!

JILL: All that straw. It's cosy.

ALAN: No.

JILL: *Why not?*

ALAN: Them!

JILL: Dalton will be in bed ... What's the matter? ... Don't you want to?

ALAN [*aching to*]: Yes!

JILL: So?

ALAN [*desperate*]: *Them! ... Them! ...*

JILL: *Who?*

ALAN [*low*]: Horses.

JILL: Horses? ... You're really dotty, aren't you? ... What do you mean?

[*He starts shaking.*]

Oh, you're freezing ... Let's get under the straw. You'll be warm there.

ALAN [*pulling away*]: No!

JILL: What on earth's the matter with you? ...

[*Silence. He won't look at her.*]

Look, if the sight of horses offends you, my lord, we can just shut the door. You won't have to see them. All right?

DYSART: What door is that? In the barn?

ALAN [*to* DYSART]: Yes.

DYSART: So what do you do? You go in?

ALAN [*to* DYSART]: Yes.

33

[*A rich light falls.*
Furtively ALAN *enters the square from the top end, and* JILL *follows.*
The horses on the circle retire out of sight on either side. NUGGET

retreats up the tunnel and stands where he can just be glimpsed in the dimness.]

DYSART: Into the Temple? The Holy of Holies?

ALAN [*to* DYSART: *desperate*]: What else can I do? . . . I can't say! I can't tell her . . . [*To* JILL.] Shut it tight.

JILL: All right . . . You're crazy.

ALAN: Lock it.

JILL: Lock?

ALAN: Yes.

JILL: It's just an old door. What's the matter with you? They're in their boxes. They can't get out . . . Are you all right?

ALAN: Why?

JILL: You look weird.

ALAN: *Lock it!*

JILL: Ssssh! D'you want to wake up Dalton? . . . Stay there, idiot.
  [*She mimes locking a heavy door, upstage.*]

DYSART: Describe the barn, please.

ALAN [*walking round it: to* DYSART]: Large room. Straw everywhere. Some tools . . . [*As if picking it up off the rail where he left it in Act One.*] A hoof pick! . . .
  [*He 'drops' it hastily, and dashes away from the spot.*]

DYSART: *Go on.*

ALAN [*to* DYSART]: At the end this big door. Behind it –

DYSART: Horses.

ALAN [*to* DYSART]: Yes.

DYSART: How many?

ALAN [*to* DYSART]: Six.

DYSART: Jill closes the door so you can't see them?

ALAN [*to* DYSART]: Yes.

DYSART: And then? . . . What happens now? . . . Come on, Alan. Show me.

JILL: See, it's all shut. There's just us . . . Let's sit down. Come on.
  [*They sit together on the same bench, left.*]
  Hallo.

ALAN [*quickly*]: Hallo.

[*She kisses him lightly. He responds. Suddenly a faint trampling of hooves, off-stage, makes him jump up.*]

JILL: What is it?

[*He turns his head upstage, listening.*]

Relax. There's no one there. Come here.

[*She touches his hand. He turns to her again.*]

You're very gentle. I love that ...

ALAN: So are you ... I mean ...

[*He kisses her spontaneously. The hooves trample again, harder. He breaks away from her abruptly towards the upstage corner.*]

JILL [*rising*]: What is it?

ALAN: Nothing!

[*She moves towards him. He turns and moves past her. He is clearly distressed. She contemplates him for a moment.*]

JILL [*gently*]: Take your sweater off.

ALAN: What?

JILL: I will, if you will.

[*He stares at her. A pause.*

She lifts her sweater over her head; he watches – then unzips his. They each remove their shoes, their socks, and their jeans. Then they look at each other diagonally across the square, in which the light is gently increasing.]

ALAN: You're ... You're very ...

JILL: So are you ... [*Pause.*] Come here.

[*He goes to her. She comes to him. They meet in the middle, and hold each other, and embrace.*]

ALAN [*to* DYSART]: She put her mouth in mine. It was lovely! *Oh, it was lovely!*

[*They burst into giggles. He lays her gently on the floor in the centre of the square, and bends over her eagerly.*

Suddenly the noise of EQUUS *fills the place. Hooves smash on wood.* ALAN *straightens up, rigid. He stares straight ahead of him over the prone body of the girl.*]

DYSART: Yes, what happened then, Alan?

ALAN [to DYSART: *brutally*]: I put it in her!

DYSART: Yes?

ALAN [to DYSART]: I put it in her.

DYSART: You did?

ALAN [to DYSART]: Yes!

DYSART: Was it easy?

ALAN [to DYSART]: Yes.

DYSART: Describe it.

ALAN [to DYSART]: I told you.

DYSART: More exactly.

ALAN [to DYSART]: I put it in her!

DYSART: Did you?

ALAN [to DYSART]: All the way!

DYSART: Did you, Alan?

ALAN [to DYSART]: All the way. I shoved it. I put it in her all the way.

DYSART: Did you?

ALAN [to DYSART]: Yes!

DYSART: Did you?

ALAN [to DYSART]: Yes! . . . Yes!

DYSART: Give me the TRUTH! . . . Did you? . . . *Honestly?*

ALAN [to DYSART]: Fuck off!

[*He collapses, lying upstage on his face.* JILL *lies on her back motionless, her head downstage, her arms extended behind her. A pause.*]

DYSART [*gently*]: What was it? You couldn't? Though you wanted to very much?

ALAN [to DYSART]: I couldn't . . . see her.

DYSART: What do you mean?

ALAN [to DYSART]: Only Him. Every time I kissed her – *He* was in the way.

DYSART: Who?

[ALAN *turns on his back.*]

ALAN [to DYSART]: You *know* who! . . . When I touched her, I felt *Him*. Under me . . . His side, waiting for my hand . . . His flanks . . . I refused him. I looked. I looked right at her. . . . and I couldn't do it. When I shut my eyes, I saw Him at once. The streaks on his belly ... [*With more desperation.*] I couldn't feel *her* flesh at all! I wanted the foam off his neck. His sweaty hide. Not flesh. *Hide! Horse-hide!* ... Then I couldn't even kiss her.

[JILL *sits up.*]

JILL: What is it?

ALAN [*dodging her hand*]: No!

[*He scrambles up and crouches in the corner against the rails, like a little beast in a cage.*]

JILL: Alan!

ALAN: Stop it!

[JILL *gets up.*]

JILL: It's all right ... It's all right ... Don't worry about it. It often happens – honest ... There's nothing wrong. I don't mind, you know ... I don't at all.

[*He dashes past her downstage.*]

Alan, look at me ... Alan? ... Alan!

[*He collapses again by the rail.*]

ALAN: Get out! ...

JILL: What?

ALAN [*soft*]: Out!

JILL: There's nothing wrong; believe me! It's very common.

ALAN: *Get out!*

[*He snatches up the invisible pick.*]

GET OUT!

JILL: Put that down!

ALAN: Leave me alone!

JILL: Put that down, Alan. It's very dangerous. Go on, please – drop it.

[*He 'drops' it, and turns from her.*]

ALAN: You ever tell anyone. Just you tell ...

JILL: Who do you think I am? ... I'm your friend – Alan ...

[*She goes towards him.*]

Listen: you don't have to do anything. Try to realize that. Nothing at all. Why don't we just lie here together in the straw. And talk.

ALAN [*low*]: Please . . .

JILL: Just talk.

ALAN: *Please!*

JILL: All right, I'm going . . . Let me put my clothes on first.

    [*She dresses, hastily.*]

ALAN: You tell anyone! . . . Just tell and see . . .

JILL: *Oh, stop it!* . . . I wish you could believe me. It's not in the least important.

    [*Pause.*]

Anyway, I won't say anything. You know that. You know I won't . . .

    [*Pause. He stands with his back to her.*]

Good night, then, Alan . . . I wish – I really wish –

    [*He turns on her, hissing. His face is distorted – possessed.*
    In horrified alarm she turns – fumbles the door open – leaves the barn –
    shuts the door hard behind her, and dashes up the tunnel out of sight,
    past the barely visible figure of NUGGET.]

34

    [ALAN *stands alone, and naked.*
    A faint humming and drumming. The boy looks about him in growing
    terror.]

DYSART: What?

ALAN [*to* DYSART]: He was there. Through the door. The door was shut, but he was there! . . . He'd seen everything. I could hear him. He was laughing.

DYSART: Laughing?

ALAN [*to* DYSART]: Mocking! . . . *Mocking!* . . .

    [*Standing downstage he stares up towards the tunnel. A great silence*
    weighs on the square.]

    [*To the silence: terrified.*] Friend . . . Equus the Kind . . . The Merciful! . . . *Forgive me!* . . .

    [*Silence.*]

It wasn't me. Not really me. *Me!* ... Forgive me! ... Take me
back again! Please! ... PLEASE!

[*He kneels on the downstage lip of the square, still facing the door,
huddling in fear.*]

I'll never do it again. I swear ... I swear! ...

[*Silence.*]

[*In a moan.*] Please!!! ...

DYSART: And He? What does He say?

ALAN [*to* DYSART: *whispering*]: 'Mine! ... You're mine! ... I am
yours and you are mine!' ... Then I see his eyes. They are rolling!

[NUGGET *begins to advance slowly, with relentless hooves, down the
central tunnel.*]

'I see you. I see you. Always! Everywhere! Forever!'

DYSART: Kiss anyone and I will see?

ALAN [*to* DYSART]: Yes!

DYSART: Lie with anyone and I will see?

ALAN [*to* DYSART]: Yes!

DYSART: And you will fail! Forever and ever you will *fail!* You will
see ME – and you will FAIL!

[*The boy turns round, hugging himself in pain. From the sides two
more horses converge with* NUGGET *on the rails.*

Their hooves stamp angrily. The EQUUS *noise is heard more terribly.*]

The Lord thy God is a Jealous God. He sees you. He sees you forever and ever, Alan. He sees you! ... *He sees you!*

ALAN [*in terror*]: Eyes! ... White eyes – never closed! Eyes like flames
– coming – coming! ... God seest! God seest! ... NO! ...

[*Pause. He steadies himself. The stage begins to blacken.*]

[*Quieter.*] No more. No more, Equus.

[*He gets up. He goes to the bench. He takes up the invisible pick. He
moves slowly upstage towards* NUGGET, *concealing the weapon behind
his naked back, in the growing darkness. He stretches out his hand and
fondles* NUGGET's *mask.*]

[*Gently.*] Equus ... Noble Equus ... Faithful and True ... Godslave ... Thou – God – Seest – NOTHING!

[*He stabs out* NUGGET's *eyes. The horse stamps in agony. A great screaming begins to fill the theatre, growing ever louder.* ALAN *dashes at the other two horses and blinds them too, stabbing over the rails. Their metal hooves join in the stamping.*

Relentlessly, as this happens, three more horses appear in cones of light: not naturalistic animals like the first three, but dreadful creatures out of nightmare. Their eyes flare – their nostrils flare – their mouths flare. They are archetypal images – judging, punishing, pitiless. They do not halt at the rail, but invade the square. As they trample at him, the boy leaps desperately at them, jumping high and naked in the dark, slashing at their heads with arms upraised.

The screams increase. The other horses follow into the square. The whole place is filled with cannoning, blinded horses – and the boy dodging among them, avoiding their slashing hooves as best he can. Finally they plunge off into darkness and away out of sight. The noise dies abruptly, and all we hear is ALAN *yelling in hysteria as he collapses on the ground – stabbing at his own eyes with the invisible pick.]*

ALAN: Find me! . . . Find me! . . . Find me! . . .

KILL ME! . . . KILL ME! . . .

35

[The light changes quickly back to brightness.

DYSART *enters swiftly, hurls a blanket on the left bench, and rushes over to* ALAN. *The boy is having convulsions on the floor.* DYSART *grabs his hands, forces them from his eyes, scoops him up in his arms and carries him over to the bench.* ALAN *hurls his arms round* DYSART *and clings to him, gasping and kicking his legs in a dreadful frenzy.*

DYSART *lays him down and presses his head back on the bench. He keeps talking – urgently talking – soothing the agony as he can.]*

DYSART: Here . . . Here . . . Ssssh . . . Ssssh . . . Calm now . . . Lie back. *Just lie back!* Now breathe in deep. Very deep. In . . . Out . . . In . . . Out . . . That's it . . . In. *Out* . . . *In* . . . Out . . .

[The boy's breath is drawn into his body with a harsh rasping sound, which slowly grows less. DYSART *puts the blanket over him.]*

Keep it going . . . That's a good boy . . . Very good boy . . . It's all over now, Alan. It's all over. He'll go away now. You'll never see him again, I promise. You'll have no more bad dreams. No more awful nights. Think of that! . . . You are going to be well. I'm going to make you well, I promise you . . . You'll be here for a while, but I'll be here too, so it won't be so bad. Just trust me . . .

[*He stands upright. The boy lies still.*]

Sleep now. Have a good long sleep. You've earned it . . . Sleep. Just sleep . . . I'm going to make you well.

[*He steps backwards into the centre of the square. The light brightens some more.*

A pause.]

DYSART: I'm lying to you, Alan. He won't really go that easily. Just clop away from you like a nice old nag. Oh, no! When Equus leaves – if he leaves at all – it will be with your intestines in his teeth. And I don't stock replacements . . . If you knew anything, you'd get up this minute and run from me fast as you could.

[HESTHER *speaks from her place.*]

HESTHER: The boy's in pain, Martin.

DYSART: Yes.

HESTHER: And you can take it away.

DYSART: Yes.

HESTHER: Then that has to be enough for you, surely? . . . In the end!

DYSART [*crying out*]: *All right! I'll take it away!* He'll be delivered from madness. *What then?* He'll feel himself acceptable! *What then?* Do you think feelings like his can be simply re-attached, like plasters? Stuck on to other objects we select? *Look at him!* . . . My desire might be to make this boy an ardent husband – a caring citizen – a worshipper of abstract and unifying God. My achievement, however, is more likely to make a ghost! . . . Let me tell you exactly what I'm going to do to him!

[*He steps out of the square and walks round the upstage end of it, storming at the audience.*]

I'll heal the rash on his body. I'll erase the welts cut into his mind by flying manes. When that's done, I'll set him on a nice miniscooter and send him puttering off into the Normal world where animals are treated *properly*: made extinct, or put into servitude, or tethered all their lives in dim light, just to feed it! I'll give him the good Normal world where we're tethered beside them – blinking our nights away in a non-stop drench of cathode-ray over our shrivelling heads! I'll take away his Field of Ha Ha, and give him Normal places for his ecstasy – multi-lane highways driven through the guts of cities, extinguishing Place altogether, *even the idea of Place!* He'll trot on his metal pony tamely through the concrete evening – and one thing I promise you: he will never touch hide again! With any luck his private parts will come to feel as plastic to him as the products of the factory to which he will almost certainly be sent. Who knows? He may even come to find sex funny. Smirky funny. Bit of grunt funny. Trampled and furtive and entirely in control. Hopefully, he'll feel nothing at his fork but Approved Flesh. *I doubt, however, with much passion! . . . Passion,* you see, can be destroyed by a doctor. It cannot be created.

[*He addresses* ALAN *directly, in farewell.*]

You won't gallop any more, Alan. Horses will be quite safe. You'll save your pennies every week, till you can change that scooter in for a car, and put the odd 50p on the gee-gees, quite forgetting that they were ever anything more to you than bearers of little profits and little losses. You will, however, be without pain. More or less completely without pain.

[*Pause.*

He speaks directly to the theatre, standing by the motionless body of ALAN STRANG, *under the blanket.*]

And now for me it never stops: that voice of Equus out of the cave – 'Why Me? . . . Why Me? . . . Account for Me!' . . . All right – I surrender! I say it! . . . In an ultimate sense I cannot know what I do in this place – yet I do ultimate things. Essentially I cannot know what I do – yet I do essential things. Irreversible, terminal things. I stand in the dark with a pick in my hand, striking at heads!

[*He moves away from* ALAN, *back to the downstage bench, and finally sits.*]

I need – more desperately than my children need me – a way of *blind horse* seeing in the dark. What way is this? . . . *What dark is this?* . . . I cannot call it ordained of God: I can't get that far. I will however *Athen* pay it so much homage. There is now, in my mouth, this sharp *horse* chain. And it never comes out.

   [*A long pause.*
   DYSART *sits staring.*]

              BLACKOUT

READ MORE IN PENGUIN

In every corner of the world, on every subject under the sun, Penguin represents quality and variety – the very best in publishing today.

For complete information about books available from Penguin – including Puffins, Penguin Classics and Arkana – and how to order them, write to us at the appropriate address below. Please note that for copyright reasons the selection of books varies from country to country.

In the United Kingdom: Please write to *Dept. JC, Penguin Books Ltd, FREEPOST, West Drayton, Middlesex UB7 0BR*

If you have any difficulty in obtaining a title, please send your order with the correct money, plus ten per cent for postage and packaging, to *PO Box No. 11, West Drayton, Middlesex UB7 0BR*

In the United States: Please write to *Penguin USA Inc., 375 Hudson Street, New York, NY 10014*

In Canada: Please write to *Penguin Books Canada Ltd, 10 Alcorn Avenue, Suite 300, Toronto, Ontario M4V 3B2*

In Australia: Please write to *Penguin Books Australia Ltd, 487 Maroondah Highway, Ringwood, Victoria 3134*

In New Zealand: Please write to *Penguin Books (NZ) Ltd,182–190 Wairau Road, Private Bag, Takapuna, Auckland 9*

In India: Please write to *Penguin Books India Pvt Ltd, 706 Eros Apartments, 56 Nehru Place, New Delhi 110 019*

In the Netherlands: Please write to *Penguin Books Netherlands B.V., Keizersgracht 231 NL–1016 DV Amsterdam*

In Germany: Please write to *Penguin Books Deutschland GmbH, Friedrichstrasse 10–12, W–6000 Frankfurt/Main 1*

In Spain: Please write to *Penguin Books S. A., C. San Bernardo 117–6^0 E–28015 Madrid*

In Italy: Please write to *Penguin Italia s.r.l., Via Felice Casati 20, I–20124 Milano*

In France: Please write to *Penguin France S. A., 17 rue Lejeune, F–31000 Toulouse*

In Japan: Please write to *Penguin Books Japan, Ishikiribashi Building, 2–5–4, Suido, Bunkyo-ku, Tokyo 112*

In Greece: Please write to *Penguin Hellas Ltd, Dimocritou 3, GR–106 71 Athens*

In South Africa: Please write to *Longman Penguin Southern Africa (Pty) Ltd, Private Bag X08, Bertsham 2013*

BY THE SAME AUTHOR

Amadeus

Winner of the *Evening Standard* Drama Award as best play of 1979, and of the *Plays and Players'* London Theatre Critics' Award

'*Amadeus* may be a play inspired by music and death, but it fills the theatre with that mocking, heavenly silence that is the overwhelming terror of life' – *The New York Times*

'Shaffer works out his tremendous, his colossal, theme in language of great strength ... those who go to it prepared to understand what it is about will have an experience that far transcends even its considerable value as drama' – Bernard Levin

'A marvellously engrossing and often amusing comic thriller, a feast for the eye and the ear ...' – Steve Grant in the *Observer*

also published

Lettice and Lovage and **Yonadab**
The Royal Hunt of the Sun

Four Plays
The Private Ear/The Public Eye;
White Liars; *Black Comedy*